TWO TRUTHS IN MY POCKET

Keep two truths in your pocket, and take them out according to the need of the moment. Let one be: For my sake was the world created. And the other: I am dust and ashes.

Rabbi Simcha Bunam
Eighteenth Century

BY LOIS RUBY

TWO TRUTHS IN MY POCKET

THE VIKING PRESS, NEW YORK

For the generations
of teachers like
Rabbi David Rose

First Edition
Copyright © 1982 by Lois Ruby
All rights reserved
First published in 1982 by The Viking Press
625 Madison Avenue, New York, New York 10022
Published simultaneously in Canada by Penguin Books Canada Limited
Printed in U.S.A.
1   2   3   4   5   86   85   84   83   82

Library of Congress Cataloging in Publication Data
Ruby, Lois.   Two truths in my pocket.
Contents: Inscriptions on stone—Forgetting me,
remember me—Lighter than air—[etc.]
1. Jews—United States—Juvenile fiction.
2. Children's stories, American. [1. Jews—United
States—Fiction. 2. Short stories] I. Title.
·PZ7.R8314Tw   [Fic]   81–70401
ISBN 0–670–73724–0   AACR2

CONTENTS

Grateful acknowledgment is made to the Central Conference of American Rabbis for permission to quote from Gates of Repentance, *edited by Chaim Stern, copyright © 1975 by the Central Conference of American Rabbis, New York, and the Union of Liberal and Progressive Synagogues, London.*

INSCRIPTIONS ON STONE

M IKE WASN'T HIS REAL NAME, NO, OR MICHAEL EITHER.
His name was Micah, which means "like unto the Lord," and
it suited him just fine in Denver. All his friends had names
that meant "God is my judge," and "God is my strength," and
"God's gracious gift." All the guys he knew wore skullcaps to
public school, from the time they were in kindergarten right
up till now, in high school.

But no one in all of Middlebury, Vermont (population
7000), wore a skullcap; no one but Micah Wexroth and his
father, the rabbi. And so, after their move to Vermont, the
skullcap went into his pocket each morning as soon as he

3

left for school, where Micah became Mike.

Just before his last birthday his mother had announced that he'd graduated from the boys' department to the men's department. "How did he get so tall?" she asked, amazed that she, four feet eleven, had produced a full-sized man of sixteen. And, indeed, he towered over his father as well, proof to all the world that there are still mysteries to the genes. In every other way he resembled his father, however: small dark eyes that seemed to keep so much within him, and brown unmown hair, and nails that grew in square and split. Even in this he was like his father: the bits of beard he found thickening on his cheeks and chin came in red. "Eric the Red and his son Derrick," his mother would joke. "Like Mazel and Schlimazel." As a child his nose had been ungainly, but his face and body had grown into it, and now even his sister reluctantly admitted that he didn't look too terribly bad.

The first day of school he was like a museum piece. Middlebury was not used to newcomers, particularly those with bits of red beard.

"Where you from, Mike?" one sandy-haired boy asked in his broad Vermont twang.

"From Denver," Micah replied.

"Denver, *Colorado*?" a girl asked.

"What other Denver is there?" Micah asked, annoyed.

"That's a long way across, isn't it?"

And Micah thought, They're so provincial in these Vermont hills they can't believe there's a whole rest of the nation out there.

4

"What're you doing here in Middlebury, Mike?" one girl asked.

He'd never lived among gentiles before. Instinctively he felt he should be guarded in his response. "My father's work. We moved here because of his job."

"Is he with the plant, then?"

"Uh, no."

"The college?"

"No, not the college, either."

They glanced from one to another. What else would bring a man and his family all the way from Denver, Colorado, to Vermont? "What does your father do, Mike?" There was a Yankee challenge to the question.

"He's a rabbi."

There was a buzz of conversation, then a question from the huddle. "What's a rabbi, exactly?"

"A teacher, a—religious leader, a spiritual leader, a—a—"

"Oh, like a Jewish minister."

"Yes." He sighed, a bit relieved.

"Curious," one girl said.

"I didn't know there were Jews in Middlebury," said another.

Actually, there were not many. Joseph Wexroth took the post in Middlebury for that reason. Burlington had three synagogues, but the Jews in the long stretch between Burlington and Bennington had no synagogue, no rabbi. Some sixty families organized loosely and combed the area for an inexpensive building. In Middlebury they found an abandoned church with small stained-glass windows depicting Old Testament stories. It was suitable. They built a simple pine Ark, put one old Torah scroll in it, and installed a Ner Tamid, an everlasting light. Then they began the search for a traditional rabbi.

Joseph Wexroth, at age forty-six, had had two coronaries. The Orthodox rabbinic organization found him Middlebury, where he could teach a small flock and study, which was his first love. Middlebury was close to the mountains, the part of Denver Rabbi Wexroth needed most, and he knew that in Vermont they'd be able to find a large old house (he didn't trust new houses), where he could shelve his library of five thousand books.

His children, Micah and Chava, going into their junior and freshman years, opposed the move loudly, but they went, of course. His wife, Miriam, promptly consulted an architect in Denver for plans to build a *mikveh* adjoining the converted church. And the rabbi occupied himself during his family's turmoil by individually wrapping and packing his books with his gentle, square hands, as though the books were made of antique glass.

Micah came home after the first day of school and reported, "Some girl in my class thinks we're curious."

His father, peering over his glasses, smiled. "We are curious, Micah, very curious. We are diamonds in a mine of zircons. High morality is always regarded as curious."

"Boy, I never felt so different in my life." Chava pouted. She was tiny, like a gymnast. "I liked it better when we were just like everyone else."

"You were *never* just like everyone else," Rabbi Wexroth said, his forehead knotted. "You are not cut from the same cloth, you and your classmates."

Miriam Wexroth carried a tray of hot chocolate and honey cookies. "What's this, Joseph—a lecture?"

"Everything Dad says is a lecture."

"Micah, tsk," his mother whispered. Miriam, who had been unreasonably sheltered as a child, had grown into a sheltering woman. She shielded first her husband, who needed it most, and then her son, and then her daughter. "While the chocolate's hot, drink. Go on, it's okay. We're having a dairy supper."

Chava groaned. "I'm tired of tuna fish and eggs and cheese, Mama. Too much cholesterol."

"Cholesterol, huh! Compared to a piece of meat?"

"I'd rather have the meat," Micah said.

"Fine. Find me a kosher butcher shop and you'll have meat."

"Didn't you see the kosher butcher? Right between the ski shop and the Congregational church," Chava teased.

"Very funny, miss. Joseph, she's a riot, your daughter."

"Tomorrow, my dear, we'll drive to New Hampshire. I hear there's a butcher shop there. Where was it, Miriam?"

"Manchester. We'll get an early start in the morning so we can be back before sundown. Tomorrow afternoon, Chavila, we pluck a fat chicken for the Sabbath. It's been—how many?—three weeks without a chicken?"

"I can wait another three to pluck, thank you."

"Joseph, there's a spot on your bifocals. Here, give me."

7

Though he protested, she was already reaching for his glasses and lifting her skirt to shine them. "Is your sermon done for Rosh Hashanah?"

"He just delivered it, Ma," Micah said. "It was about the Chosen People, a cut above, diamonds in the mine—that sermon."

"Show a little respect, Micah."

"Mama, guess what. They call him Mike in school."

"Mike!" his father shouted.

"We'll talk about it later, Joseph."

"Micah is a worthy name, a prophet, a righteous man. You can do better with Mike?"

"It's only a name, Dad."

After a few weeks at school, it seemed that everyone had forgotten about his father being a rabbi. And once that was forgotten, it was also easy to forget that Micah was Jewish, different.

He got to be friends with a boy more worldly than the others, who'd lived in Boston until he was twelve. His name was Savvy Larcher. He was big, built. His shoulders had broadened from summer carpentry, and his forearms were full and veined like a much older man's. There his development ended, as if he'd been half-built before they ran out of materials. From the waist down, he was shapeless: thin thighs (his gym shorts hung all around them) and almost feminine ankles. Micah thought Savvy looked like a paraplegic, with all muscle and tone in the top half of him. But Chava thought he was cute and hinted that she might like to date him.

8

"Date him!" her father yelled. "If he had twice as much sense, he would be an idiot."

"You don't like Savvy because he's not Jewish," Micah said.

"I don't like him because he's a *nebesh*, a nothing."

"Come to think of it, Deano Murray is cuter anyway. He has a moped," Chava said.

"Oy, Murray yet. Why not Kelly or O'Leary?"

"Well, there sure aren't any Rosenbergs around, Daddy. I'm doing the best I can."

Savvy drove a pickup truck. Rabbi Wexroth had a 1950's suspicion of pickups. "You're not riding in that—that machine, Micah."

"What's the matter with it? It runs better than your 1969 Ford. Savvy keeps it up. Savvy and Joe, they're good mechanics, tops."

"You're not going to ride in it, period."

"I am."

Then his father would open a book and leave the air hanging heavy.

So Micah would jog around the block, and Savvy would cruise with his headlights off and pick Micah up. One night in early November Savvy and Joe and Micah drove out to a hut in the country that featured hamburgers, cheap. Micah had made excuses about the food for two months. But now, at Cleo's, the aroma of good, bloody meat frying on the grill, blending with a whole day's worth of forbidden foods—the aroma overtook him, and Micah ate his first non-kosher hamburger.

9

He suspected he might be unable to swallow, and if he swallowed, he'd surely choke. And if he choked, he'd be found dead in Cleo's Hamburger Hell-O, and his father would claim the body and would turn white with unexploded anger.

"This meat tastes like shoe leather," Joe said.

"Shoe leather. That's too complimentary," Savvy said. "Tastes more like a cement patio that's just been poured."

Micah nodded in agreement but found the hamburger gloriously delicious. He swallowed it in four bites, wishing he had another fifty cents so he could order a second one. Maybe a cheeseburger.

The smell of the hamburger boiling in the accumulated greases of the grill stayed with him all evening, stayed on his hands, stayed in slippery places around his mouth, until he got home and suddenly felt nauseous.

"Chava, get out of the bathroom, quick!"

"What's the matter with you?" she yelled through the bathroom door. "Did you have an enema? You and Savvy treat yourselves to an enema tonight?"

"I'm warning you, get out!"

She opened the door, with a towel wrapped around her head, saw his pasty face, and quickly ran out.

Sitting on the toilet, his body contorted with stomach cramps, Micah promised himself anything for relief. No more sneaking around to Savvy's truck. No more Cleo's Hamburger Hell-O. He'd even go back to being called Micah, though now it seemed like a name for a different person, a person who wore a tiny knitted skullcap and argued with rabbis and scholars about Talmudic law; a person so wholly absorbed in praying on Saturday mornings that he did not notice if other men still stood around him in the synagogue. That was the person who'd never had stomach cramps, not once in his life.

No more Savvy's truck, no more Savvy, no more non-kosher meat. No more.

But as the last wave of pain passed, the righteous moment of resolution passed as well. He washed his hands and phoned Savvy.

"Hey, Mike," Savvy said, all excited. "Joe and I have this wild, wild idea. I've been cooking it up in my lab, my private lab in my brain. Tomorrow night we'll drive over to Widow's Peak, to the ski resort there, you know?"

"What for? It's a long ride, maybe thirty miles."

"It's worth it. Wait till you hear this plan." Savvy paused. "Is anybody listening?"

"No, they're all in their own holes."

"Then listen to *this*."

At dinner the next night Micah announced he had plans for the evening.

"Where are you going, darling?" his mother asked absently. "To the library, maybe? A school club meeting?"

"Just somewhere with my friends."

"Friends," his father said with measured contempt. "You lie down with dogs, you rise with fleas."

Chava said, "Donald Gordon asked me to a movie. Can I go, Daddy?"

"No."

"Don't be too hasty, Joseph. The girl is fifteen. In ninth grade they go out already."

The phone rang. Micah and Chava raced for it, but Micah won. He came back to the table with a smirk on his face. "It's for *Eva*," he said.

"Eva?" her father said.

Chava blushed. "Well, it's the English translation, Daddy."

"Um-hum. And soon instead of Rabbi they can call me Reverend Wexroth."

"It's a guy named Donald. Donald Gordon," Micah shouted.

"Shut up, Micah."

"This is the dinner table. Tell him to call back."

"Oh, Ma, no."

"Your mother said."

Micah couldn't eat. He was reviewing the plans for Widow's Peak. They would each chip in a dollar for gas, drive out there. No one would be there, a week before the ski season was to open. They'd scale the fence—

"You're not eating, Micah," his mother pointed out.

"Is that a capital offense?"

"If you can't talk to your mother with respect, swallow your words."

"Thank you, Joseph."

"He'll never call back, I know it."

"Donald Gordon will call back, believe me," Mrs. Wexroth said. She glanced nervously at her husband, but he was absorbed in some logical argument in his head and was fueling it with rhythmic bites of everything on his plate, mixed together into a mush.

—they'd scale the fence. Savvy had a book on picking locks. He'd studied for this, prepared for it. He'd get them into the sentry box where the gondolas up to the ski slopes were controlled. Micah looked at his watch, listened for ticking; it was moving so slowly.

The phone rang again. Donald was calling back, five minutes later. Micah answered the phone and left. He'd wait for Savvy around the corner, either that or explode at the dinner table.

Savvy and Joe picked him up. Savvy seemed agitated, like a nervous Siamese cat. Joe, a runt with one blue and one gray eye, and a mop of curly blond hair, kept telling jokes to calm Savvy. If he'd been a girl, he'd have been massaging Savvy's back, but the jokes would do.

"What's tall, green, and dances?"

"I dunno—what?" Savvy bit his cuticles raw.

"You know, Mike?"

"I give up."

"Fred Asparagus!"

"I don't get it," Savvy said, distracted. He'd never driven this far before, and not at night.

"Fred Astaire, Fred *Asparagus!*"

"Who the hell is Fred Astaire?"

"Some dancer," Micah replied. "Old."

"Okay, Sav, here's another one. How do you get twenty-one Jews in a Volkswagen?"

Micah stiffened, but bit his lip. He'd go along with the joke. It was only a joke.

"I dunno—how?" Savvy asked. His foot tapped the accelerator as if he were playing the drums.

"Easy. One in the back seat and twenty in the ashtray."

Savvy rewarded Joe with a burst of laughter. It was only a joke. Micah laughed too, a tin sound to his laughter. Only a joke.

"One in the back seat, twenty in the ashtray!" Joe repeated, trying for further mileage.

"Okay, now let me concentrate on the road."

Joe, as always, obeyed, and the three bounced along in silence. Widow's Peak was ahead, snow from last year still painted on its tip. There would have to be a couple of great snowfalls for the season to open on schedule next week. Micah could sense snow in the air. There was a sharp thinness, as though the atmosphere were ready to crack. Snow would fall within minutes. Birds, those few that were left, did not linger on the fence posts any more, but hurried, as his mother had when she'd prepared them all to leave Denver. There was a mist, but not a mist, more a tingle that touched the skin of his upper lip and warned that soon he would lick snowflakes from it.

"It's not going to snow tonight," Savvy announced, like a royal proclamation. Joe, who believed Savvy had a direct line, agreed.

But Micah knew. There would be snow, and there would be a thin sheet of ice on the twisting mountain ride home. And this was Savvy's first winter driving. I hope we make it home all right, Micah prayed silently.

In Denver he'd been in the habit of having conversations with God, in his head. They'd been out of touch since the move. He'd mentioned it to Chava once. She'd said God just hadn't gotten the new address. Too many people moved over the summer. There was a backlog, like in the courts. So Micah was surprised to hear the soundless voice in his head.

"You're asking Me to help you make it home?"

"Well, yes."

"Hmph."

The response was familiar. Micah waited for the barrage.

"Did you talk to Me this morning when you woke up? In fact, have you said word one to Me lately? A few blasphemies, maybe."

"I've been busy."

"So I see."

"Is it going to snow on our road home?"

"You've always been able to tell about snow."

"I'm asking *You.*"

"I don't answer questions."

"No, or prayers, either."

"I've got it!" Savvy yelled. He opened the door of the control booth.

"Sh. There could be a night watchman," Joe whispered, but reverently. His face glowed with excitement: the adventure, yes, but mostly his pride in Savvy's tremendous accomplishment.

And Micah heard in his head, "Are you sure you know what you're doing?"

"It's a boyish prank, as my mother would say. Harmless. I'm just having a good time with my friends."

"Friends?" Then, a voice more like his father's than God's said, "If you don't eat garlic, you won't smell."

"Right here, right *here*, Joe. The screwdriver, right here."

Joe pulled a pocket-sized screwdriver from his jeans and loosened a few knobs on the control panel.

Micah knew nothing about machinery, and so he knew nothing about how to trip it up. He stood and examined the darkness for a headlight, footsteps, the smell of a watchdog. Watching, waiting—he knew these from the tradition of his forefathers. Savvy, on his back, reached up to disconnect a wire. Joe stuck his sneaker in Savvy's armpit, Savvy shot up, bumped his head, swore.

"Sh, someone's coming," Micah warned. Tiny flakes of snow bounced off a set of headlights growing larger.

"Quick, out of here pronto," Savvy commanded. They darted behind some evergreens a few yards from the control booth. Savvy, in a light jeans jacket, shivered and bit his cuticles. Joe pulled up his hooded wool plaid coat, zipped it up to his lower lip. Micah crouched behind the tree until his foot went to sleep and shot pins up his leg. He couldn't move. His skullcap fell out of his pocket, but he didn't dare reach for it.

A night watchman played his flashlight around the control booth, cocked his head as if he heard something, shot around,

16

shone the light on the trees. Joe and his red plaid were flat on the ground. Micah and Savvy melted into the darkness; the only movement near them was snowflakes bouncing off the points of pine needles.

"Anybody there?" the watchman asked.

A chipmunk, the last of the season, came out to stare at the watchman, then scurried away with berries in its front paws. The man whirled around at the movement, terror plainly on his face. "Ho," he sighed, relieved, and walked toward his car. His rubber boots mashed the thin snow like cereal crumbs on a kitchen floor. He drove off.

Savvy was shivering.

"Hey, you okay?" Joe asked.

"J-j-just cold. Give me your coat a minute, will you?"

Joe considered it. "Why should I freeze, too?"

"Thanks. I knew I could count on you," Savvy sneered, as Micah took off his down jacket. "Thanks," Savvy said gruffly.

Micah wasn't cold; he could control the cold, except for his ears. His ears were stinging, like his foot.

"Let's get out of here," Savvy said. "We've done a thorough job already. Joe, go lock up. Take your gloves off for thirty seconds and lock up. Mike, wipe his nose, will you?"

Micah heard his own hollow laugh echo through the still night. He started up the road to the pickup, which was hidden behind some trees. He glanced over his shoulder at Savvy, who was shaking like the pine branches, even with the down coat zipped around him. Micah suddenly wanted to run, not to the truck but all the way home, to Denver, to Mr. Sandler.

Mr. Sandler taught Talmud Torah, three afternoons a week to the boys who used to be all of Micah's world. They used to argue with Mr. Sandler, knowing an argument with Mr. Sandler was an exercise in futility. He had them on every point, could quote from masters they hadn't read yet, and what he couldn't quote he made up and made it sound ancient.

"I could be on the swimming team, but instead here I sit every sunny afternoon," one of the boys would grumble. "How come it doesn't rain on the days we have Hebrew school?"

"When you're young, you study," Mr. Sandler said.

"But you're an old man—you still study. Is this what I've got to look forward to?"

"An old man studies too, harder."

"Whew, what a life. When do you get to live it?"

"In between the pages. It's all there. You step out of the synagogue, everything you've read is right there on East Hanover Street, and if not, you'll turn a corner and you'll find the rest. Gentlemen, both places you learn. Out there you learn it with a *klop* to the head, an agony in the heart. Here you learn it first."

The boys groaned. It was an act. They believed Mr. Sandler knew all the secrets of the universe, and that, given enough time, he would impart the mysteries to them. And then he held them with this: by tradition they could not explore the mystical books of the Kabbalah until they were twenty-five. They had to stay with him, study with Mr. Sandler until they could sample the forbidden fruit.

18

"Aw, Mr. Sandler, it's too hot to study today."

"You are here to learn of The One Without End. You will study." He pierced them with his small dark eyes, raised a hand, three fingers missing, and waved it gracefully in the air. He charged the air for them. The mystery of his lost fingers would be the first revealed. "Did I ever say this before? Listen. Ibn Gabirol, in the eleventh century, said something you should all copy down in your notebooks." (They had written it down, in Hebrew and English, at least half a dozen times, and wrote again.) " 'To seek wisdom in old age is like a mark in the sand; to seek wisdom in youth is like an inscription on stone.' What, Ezra, you write faster than a mortal?" And Ezra, dreaming, would begin to scribble, as Mr. Sandler repeated the message in Hebrew.

Seek wisdom when you're young. Yes, and Micah had learned a number of new things tonight. He'd learned to crack a lock, to search the night with fear, to crouch like a hunted animal, to refuse to be cold, even as the snow fell all around him.

Then, with no heat in the truck, and snow crusting the windshield, and the dark mountain road frosting in unsuspected patches; with very little tread on the tires, and Savvy unable to stop shivering, and Joe munching corn nuts and telling jokes between teeth caked with wet crumbs, Micah rode home to the house of his father.

A waterfall ran through the center of Middlebury. Past the small department store with fading window displays, and the bookstore, and the five-and-ten stocked with toys no longer manufactured and gnarled ribbons and Dr. Scholl's foot preparations, the rush of freezing waters could be heard. Across the street from the one movie house in town—a waterfall.

Chava and Micah stood at the stone wall overlooking the violent waters that rushed beneath and between the buildings of-Middlebury.

"He'll find out, Micah. What will you do when he finds out?"

"He won't find out."

"It's in the newspapers, Micah. It even made the Burlington paper."

"He doesn't read the papers."

"No, but Mama reads to him. Well, at least your name isn't mentioned in the paper. Yet," she added under her breath.

"Did today's paper say how he is, that man from Widow's Peak?" Micah asked.

"No, only that he was badly electrocuted. He's in the hospital."

"I know, I know."

"If you know, why did you ask?"

"I just don't understand it. How could it have happened? It was just supposed to be for fun. We were just supposed to stop the ski lift, not hurt anyone."

"The paper said someone tampered with the wires."

"Yes, I know."

"That was pretty stupid, Micah."

For two days the equipment inspector had lain in the

hospital. There were reports of heart and liver damage, and that his hair had turned completely white from the jolt of electricity he'd received.

A woman passed them, clutching her coat collar closed with one hand, a newspaper with the other. Micah imagined that everyone suspected him. The woman smiled, and Micah tried to guess if the smile meant she *knew*. He wanted to shout at her, at the roar of the waterfall, "I'm responsible. The accident at Widow's Peak, I'm the one who caused it. The man with the white hair, all of it. It's my fault."

"I don't know what will happen when Daddy finds out. He could have another heart attack. Oh, Micah."

"You're really encouraging."

"He expects so much from us, you know. From you especially, the only son."

"I'm not what he expects."

"Does he know? Not about Widow's Peak. About the other thing?"

"I haven't been able to tell him yet. I've tried, really. But nine generations of rabbis. How can I tell him I'm breaking the chain? He wrote the Yeshiva already."

"Micah, I've been thinking." She paused, her eyes darting to her brother. "The chain isn't necessarily broken." She fingered the leather fringe on her purse, pulled her coat tighter around her. Her lips were chapped, stayed chapped all winter, just as a knot of cold settled into her flesh and didn't leave until spring. "Not necessarily."

"Oh? You've got plans for me, also?"

"For me."

"You?" Micah stared at his sister. Somewhere between Denver and Middlebury, she'd grown up, rounded, thinned. Before, she'd taken choppy steps, as though all she ever wore were clogs. Now he noticed, as she paced the narrow bridge, that the wide hems of her slacks swayed gracefully over her boots.

"I will be the—rabbi," she said.

He wanted to laugh, wanted to tell her she couldn't, no one would let her, she wouldn't pass the physical, she couldn't touch the Torah, she was—less than a man.

But something in the set of her face, in the way she never blinked while he studied her face, a gesture of her hands that seemed so full of knowing, like a benediction, told him he was wrong.

"The problem now, though," Chava continued, "is that you have to find a way to tell him you won't, and I have to find a way to tell him I will. Neither will please him, you know."

Pleasing him had always been their main concern. It had been Micah's purpose, his sister's, his mother's. The rabbi did not demand it of them; they had simply offered it. The man had a faith so resolute that his family could not tolerate the pain of his disillusionment. Yet, Micah wondered, was his father's faith so strong, really, if they all had to protect him from doubt? Whom were they shielding? The earth was always firm under Rabbi Wexroth, but under his wife? His children?

When Micah first read about the man's whitening hair, he considered how he might atone privately; his father must never know. He would do the thing expected of him: study, obey, teach, preach, as the fathers and grandfathers before him had. His rabbinate would be his repentance, and if the man in the hospital should not live, Micah would be all the more committed to the choice. Yes, he had decided, and he welcomed the heavy burden.

That afternoon he picked up his old notebooks from Mr. Sandler's class. He would begin his study immediately. "A man should believe he is reborn each day," the notebook read. Well, Micah would be reborn this day. He would find joy in his decision. Then the notebook fell open to a saying from the Talmud, "Live by the commandments; do not die by them."

Could he live by them, locked into a destiny not his own?

He slid the notebook under his bed and held his face in his hands until his back ached. Darkness fell. He had no idea how many hours passed. At times he forgot where he was. And finally he decided to risk shaking his father's faith. He would tell his father tonight.

But two days later, as he stood with Chava by the surging waters, he had not yet spoken to his father.

Friday night Rabbi Wexroth and his wife sat in back-to-back chairs, reading by one lamp. Her book was modern, his less so. The radio was tuned to an FM station, where it would stay until the Sabbath was over at sundown Saturday. A Tchaikovsky symphony played, barely audible. Chava hugged her knees, listening to the music, but in her mind the music kept dissolving into football cheers and shouts from the coach at the sideline: "Hey, Screwhead, grab 'im. What a team. *What* a team!" She forced Tchaikovsky back.

Micah slid his skullcap back and forth over his head, tried to figure geometry problems without a pencil. On the Sabbath one did not write. The phone rang. Chava jumped. It couldn't be Donald Gordon. Donald would be at the football game. Who, then?

Mrs. Wexroth looked up from her book, glanced behind her at her husband, returned to her reading. Micah saw the words and symbols swim on the page. Each time the phone had rung since Widow's Peak, he had felt a wave of panic overtake him. Maybe they'd figured it out. Maybe they'd found out it was Savvy's truck, and Savvy would send them to him, even though he had given Savvy his coat that night. How could his parents sit there when the phone kept ringing? How could he, Micah's father, not even hear it?

Eight rings, and still Rabbi Wexroth was undisturbed, reading a book with thick yellowed pages. Micah imagined he was a time traveler, and there was a man and a book from a century before, superimposed on the exact spot that he and the telephone occupied. The man would not hear the phone; he had lived in this room before phones were invented. Nor would he see Micah if Micah walked in front of him. They could not exist at the same time.

"Can't we answer the phone, Daddy, just this once?"

Her mother replied, "It's the Sabbath, Chavila."

They returned to their books and the music, and Chava speculated on who might be phoning her. Reluctantly she admitted to herself that it was nearly more fun guessing than knowing. The mystery of Sabbath was guessing what the gentile world was doing, while they alone, in all of Middlebury, celebrated the creation of life by withdrawing from the activity all around them.

Then later someone rang the doorbell. A person at the door—this was more imperative than a phone call. Chava and Micah raced to the door. Two policemen stood there. The taller one, who wore a sparse mustache that did not cover a lip scar, asked, "Are you Michael Wexroth?"

"Micah, yes."

Chava took his arm.

The other policeman, much older, coarser, asked, "Your father here?" He was flashing his identification papers like a checkered flag.

"You can't talk to him right now," Chava said. "He won't talk to you."

"What is it?" Mrs. Wexroth came to the door, saw the policemen. She looked around her, a quick inventory. Yes, her family was all safe, thank God. "What happened?"

"Your husband here?" the older policeman asked.

"Joseph!"

Nothing disturbed the rabbi's reverie on the Sabbath. But he knew, the way his wife called his name, that he must go at once.

"You Mr. Wexroth?"

"*Rabbi* Wexroth," his wife corrected the taller man.

"Rabbi? Well, listen, Rabbi, your kid's in a mess, your son."

Mrs. Wexroth looked at Micah, disbelieving. "It's a mistake, officer. My son's been here all evening. What is it?"

"Rabbi, you and your boy better come down to the station."

"But he can't!" Mrs. Wexroth cried. "He won't ride on the Sabbath." She stood in front of her husband, her arms outstretched, as though she were shielding a child from flames.

"It's all right, Miriam—we'll walk," her husband said gently. "Micah, go and get your coat. Miriam, my coat and hat from the closet." His wife stared at him. More firmly he said, "My coat, Miriam." She nodded, brought his coat, and helped him on with it, while Chava, waiting for tears, handed her father his hat. He removed his skullcap, folded it neatly into a triangle, and put it in his pocket. He arranged his hat in front of the hall mirror, straightening his tie also. "Come, son," he said simply.

"Joseph." Mrs. Wexroth clung to her husband.

He gently moved her away. "It's all right, my dear."

"But a policeman comes to our door, tells us nothing," she whispered to her husband.

"They've always come for us in the night." He sighed. "Go to bed, Chavila, it's late."

Chava watched her father, a small man with a ridiculous hat, walk down the driveway. Her tears began when the police car quickly overtook him.

A rabbi's integrity is unquestioned, even in a gentile community. Micah was released, without bail, on his father's word. While lawyers worked through the tangled threads of the

Widow's Peak incident, Micah went home to await the trial. He wished he had not. Or that his father would explode in anger, demand to know why Micah had allowed himself to stray so far from Mr. Sandler's teachings. Instead his father offered him a quiet acceptance, as though he no longer cared why.

If there had been bail, borrowed or mortgaged, how much better. To be released on his father's four-thousand-year-old reputation—this was too difficult for the boy who searched his father's dark, hidden eyes for a reflection of the man's disillusionment. And searching, he found none. Only quiet acceptance, such as Micah had seen on that Yom Kippur morning in 1973 when his father had explained to the congregation how Israel had been prodded out of its synagogues into war.

Rabbi Wexroth caught the flu. It settled in his throat and chest and saved him from speaking to his son.

"Joseph, look. Even in New England there's cough medicine. This will fix your throat in a minute. Also hot tea with honey and lemon. Believe me, it cures!"

How jovial his mother tried to be. But her voice changed, though nearly imperceptibly, when she spoke to Micah. "Are you going back to school tomorrow, darling? You missed a week already. It's time to go back."

"I guess so." He didn't want to go back, face the questions, watch Savvy bite his cuticles until they bled.

His mother glanced from her husband to her son. "Well, I'll leave you two alone," she said cheerily.

"Dad?"

His father made a guttural sound, took a mouthful of the steaming tea. "Yes?"

"I'm making other plans."

"What plans?"

"For after I graduate."

"This I know."

"You know? That I'm not going to the Yeshiva?"

"I'm not blind." His voice was hoarse. He again sipped the tea.

"No, you've never been blind. You've just always been—"

"What?"

"So sure. Sure you were right."

His father smiled, a sad look in his eyes. "Yet how wrong I was."

And the remark, though innocently given, stung. "Well, there's no law that says I have to follow in your footsteps."

"Law? You talk to me of law?" He pushed the tea away and closed his eyes.

"Well, anyway, I just want you to know. When this whole mess is cleared up, I'm going to leave."

"You have another year of high school."

"I'll go back to Denver. I can live with Mr. Sandler."

"You think Manuel Sandler runs a home for wayward boys? Never mind. What about after high school?"

"I haven't decided," he said, feeling the anger rising. His father had no right to ask him, to force him to reveal that he had no idea what he wanted to do.

"Just so you should not jump into something too fast."

"Thou shalt not," Micah thought. How many "Thou shalt nots" had his father served up to him? Had his people served up to one another for countless years? There were 613 *mitzvot*, commandments of ethics and behavior, that traditional Jews were supposed to follow. And his father had surely followed them all. How many—365?—were "Thou shalt nots."

"You should not be hasty. Decide what you want. Don't decide against what you think I want."

Micah prepared himself for another lecture, this time in the raspy voice. He can't let me go, Micah thought, without the packet of lectures and laws. It would have been easier if there had been another son to succeed his father while he, Micah, went off elsewhere. And then, for the first time, he wondered how it was that his parents had managed to have only two children in twenty years of marriage. Had they violated an Orthodox "Thou shalt not" in limiting their family? Hadn't they, as the law required, renewed their marriage each Sabbath in the privacy of their room? Micah looked at his father with a startling new interest. And did his mother direct his father there, as she did everywhere else? Did she protect him from the reality of their act when they were locked together under the white crocheted bedspread? Or was Joseph Wexroth a driving, powerful man at those times, a man like other men?

Never before had Micah thought of his father as being like any other man. He was human; like father, like son. Then, if his father was only human, Micah had a solid right to be himself, even to disappoint Joseph Wexroth, who was not an angel but a man. Micah had a right to break the chain that spanned nine generations of firstborn sons who became rabbis.

"I need a little rest," his father said.

"Yes, I'll go and let you sleep."

His father reached for the blanket weakly, silently inviting Micah to help him with it. Micah spread the blanket over him, noticing the shabby look of a day's growth on the man's face, the wool bathrobe thinning at the elbows, and a gray/maroon pattern to the pajamas beneath, half the collar tucked in, half out. Except for the skullcap, he could have been a man picked up on Skid Row: his voice raspy from wine, his legs unwilling to support him, his hands trembling with chill as the blanket is placed over him.

For two days Rabbi Wexroth slept, woke to read awhile, and fell back to sleep with his glasses on and the book open on his chest.

Chava's impatience grew, and by the third day she could wait no longer. The rest had helped the rabbi's voice, or maybe he had more voice to talk to his daughter than to his son. "Chavila."

He reached for her hand, and holding his, she said, "There were eight rabbis before you, and there will be lots more after you. I will see to it that the line isn't broken. There will be a rabbi in this generation." She held his hand tightly.

" 'The voice is the voice of Jacob, but the hands are the hands of Esau,' " her father quoted. "Do you fool me this way, pretending to me that my son will follow me?"

"I will follow you."

"Both of you are my children, like fingers on my hand. Five fingers, and no two alike, and yet a cut on one finger hurts as much as on another. You, my Chava, are not the thumb, not the index finger. You are the precious little finger."

"No, Papa."

He lifted his weary eyes to his daughter, pulled the blanket tighter around him. "Papa? I haven't heard Papa since you were in maybe first grade." They were both silent. "You'll marry one day, make a home. There will be babies."

"No, Papa."

"No babies?" he asked sternly.

"I may marry. There may be babies. But I will be a rabbi first." Even as she said it and felt it to be true, she knew how absurd it must sound to him.

"Micah is Micah, a different finger. You're not responsible for your brother."

"It has nothing to do with Micah. It's me, Chava Wexroth, Eva."

"A rabbi? My little Chava, there are no women rabbis. Do you expect to plow the field for the first time?"

"Not Orthodox women rabbis. There are others."

His eyes widened, but he said only, "I see."

"Everything you hold sacred, Papa, is sacred to me, too."

"No. We speak of two different things. My throat is dry. Please, bring me some hot tea."

"Yes, Papa." She sighed, got up, gathered his teacup and

the sticky honey spoon to return to the kitchen, while her father pulled the chain on the lamp beside him and settled into dusk.

No one sat on the benches in the town square. It was called The Green, but it had not been green for months. Micah and Chava kicked a path in the fresh snow, so clean beside the gray accumulation of winter.

"He seems to be adjusting," Chava said, her teeth chattering.

"Notice how we always call him *he*. It's a notch below His Majesty."

"There *is* something special about him, Micah. He's forty-six and so naïve. Who else could stay that way?"

"He seemed to accept our plans, no arguments. It's almost disappointing. I expected more of him."

"You're just like him. You both have too many expectations."

"I'm not like him," Micah said angrily.

"Oh, yes, Micah, very like him."

In the gray distance they saw someone, Joe. He turned the other way when he spotted them, then apparently realized he could not avoid them. In a town the size of Middlebury nothing could be avoided. "Hi, Mike," he called. His voice sounded forlorn. He wore the same wool hooded coat, zipped up to his lower lip.

"Do you know my sister, Eva?"

"Oh, yeah, I've seen her around."

The three of them stood in awkward silence. Micah, feeling

32

the sting of cold for the first time since Widow's Peak, began to walk. The others followed him. Over his shoulder he asked, "How's Savvy?"

"Oh, great, fine. His folks are moving—did you hear? To West Virginia. Jeeze, West Virginia!" His words were muffled by the coat.

"Not before the trial, are they?"

"Who knows? It could take months before the trial starts." Micah nodded.

"The guy is out of the hospital—did you hear?" Joe asked.

"I heard," Micah said.

"You know all that talk about the white hair? I saw him on TV. It wasn't white at all."

"Lucky, I guess."

"Savvy says the whole town is getting worked up over nothing. The guy is okay. It was just a couple of kids pulling a prank."

"Savvy's stupid."

"Yeah, well."

They were silent again, Chava glancing from one boy to the other. Finally Joe said, "Still, the guy could've croaked." He rubbed the little bit of his face that was showing. "He could be dead, and where would we be then?" He walked away, as though dazed.

Chava and Micah started across the street to find a place to thaw out. The Middlebury Inn was just opposite The Green, and its owners did not mind if people came in and sat by the fire in the lobby.

A menu was posted for the inn's restaurant. Featured that

day: baked cured Virginia ham and scalloped potatoes, turkey with oyster dressing—things Micah knew he would never eat.

A couple of skiers tumbled down the great staircase and rang the little bell to call someone to the desk. "There's no water in our room. The pipes are frozen shut," the young man said merrily.

The desk attendant tried to look properly sympathetic. It was a complaint she probably heard daily. "Oh, well, then, we'll just switch you to another room," Micah heard her say in the Vermont twang he barely noticed any more. "There isn't much else we can do. In the spring it'll all work out."

"Did you hear what she said?" Chava whispered. "In the spring it'll all work out. Dad will be okay, I know it."

"Always him. And what about us?"

She looked at him with surprise. "We're okay now, Micah."

Micah thought about how much easier life was—had always been—for Chava. She accepted what she could and shrugged her shoulders at the rest. She adapted. She was like their mother. But he? Micah spun the skullcap on his head, and even as he smiled with Chava, he wondered if things would always be harder for him.

FORGETTING ME, REMEMBER ME

D<small>R. TOM HORTON HAD A STROKE. I WAS AFRAID WE WERE</small> going to lose him, but he came through. My grandfather had a stroke and died. We didn't know about Dr. Tom Horton for weeks. Would he make it? Would he be stuck in place? We didn't know for weeks. My grandfather died right away. The hospital called to say so.

"But, Tracy dear," my mother said, "Grampa was real, and Tom Horton is a television actor. That's not real life, dear, that's soap opera."

But I don't believe it, because Dr. Tom Horton hasn't been the same since his stroke.

"As usual, Tracy's screwed up," my brother Alan said. He's a year younger than I am, but he's in eighth grade, and I'm not in a grade. So he thinks he's much smarter. One year, I forget when, we were in the same grade, but that was a long time ago.

Alan is getting ready for his Bar Mitzvah. My sister Vivian, who's away at college, thinks it's stupid that Alan's having a Bar Mitzvah. She never did it. I didn't, of course, because I'm in the ungraded class. But I love it that Alan is being Bar Mitzvahed. I wish it was me.

My mother rows all the time. Not on the ocean. In our family room. "Here, Tracy, try it," she always says. "It'll flatten your tummy, give some substance to those budding breasts of yours." Half the time I don't know what she's talking about, but I know she wants me to row to be as beautiful as she is. Oh, and Mama is beautiful! She wears big silver hoops in her ears. She gets her hair frosted and cut very short to a point right at the middle of her neck. She has big shoulders—from rowing, I guess—and I think the point in the middle of her neck between her shoulders goes all the way down her back in a straight line, like a skunk. Maybe not.

My hair is much longer than Mama's. It takes a long time to dry, but I wash it every night. I might cut it for the Bar Mitzvah. Julie Olson Banning Anderson Williams used to have very long hair that curled into beautiful dark things around her face. She got it cut before she married Doug, way before Dr. Tom Horton's stroke. (He's her grandfather.) She and Doug are married in real life, too, you know. I saw it in a magazine. Anyway, my hair doesn't look like Julie O.B.A.

Williams', even when hers was long. Mine is light brown and straight and thick and doesn't flip at the ends like pixie toes. Also, Julie has perfect teeth. Mine have little white spots on them.

I have a lot of health problems. It goes with being MBD. Some people don't know what MBD is. It's what they call my class at school. MBD means Minimally Brain Damaged, and we're not supposed to know that. But I know it, and it doesn't matter. When Michael Horton was a baby, he had a brain disease, and he's just fine now. Very handsome, in fact. He was born when I was five, but he's already at least twenty-two. On *Days of Our Lives* people grow up fast.

"Grow up, Spook," my brother Alan always says to me. My sister Vivian, who will be home next week for the Bar Mitzvah, thinks I'm about seven years old. But she'll see. I can wear her dresses now. They don't hang like drapes on me any more. I tried on her old senior prom dress last night, and danced in front of the mirror with my hair held up by fancy combs. I pretended I was a princess. I had rosy cheeks and eyelashes from Woolworth's. But I'm not really a princess.

"Tracy. Tra-CEE!" my father called. He has such a nice voice, like Don Pardo on TV. Only it sounds mad so many times. "Tracy Lynn, get yourself up here pronto."

I ran up the stairs. When my father calls, you run up the stairs. He doesn't have much time to waste. He was sitting in his bedroom with a silky red robe on, and cowboy boots. My father is an oil man. I think everyone in Texas is. Everyone *we* know, anyway.

39

"Tracy Lynn, you brewing up an idea about what you want to do for the Bar Mitzvah shindig?"

"I could keep the guest book?"

"Honey, you'd have 'em signing in cockeyed. Better stick to something more in your line."

I thought and thought about what was in my line. I wanted it to be something special, something no one but me could do for Alan that night. But what? I couldn't arrange flowers. I was too clumsy. My mother said Poorly Coordinated. And the flower shop could do that anyway. All the food was being brought over by Heaven Scent Caterers. I could bake, but they didn't need that. Heaven Scent baked Jewish breads and cream puffs and apple strudel.

"Tracy Lynn, come sit here by old Dad." He patted the big chair next to him. I loved the smell of the chair, and of old Dad. He smelled like something I've always known. But he was bony and not very cozy to sit next to, and the way he clenched his teeth around his pipe, I thought he might bite at any time. "Well, honey," he said, but not looking at me, "we'll find you a spot in the show." He flipped through a bunch of papers on his desk, Bar Mitzvah bills, I think. "You're pretty good at sweeping up."

I didn't want to sweep up after Alan's Bar Mitzvah. I wanted to matter *during* it. But then I saw that old Dad was smiling at his bills and he didn't mean it. Sometimes I can't tell when people are teasing, until that scared feeling around my heart lets go and I can smile along with them.

"It's Sabbath, Dad. The next Sabbath will be Alan's."

"So it's Sabbath, is it? Well, leave it to Little Miss Super Jew to remind us."

"I guess we're not lighting the candles tonight." I sighed.

My father looked up finally. "That again? Look, honey, we're not that kind of Jew. It's just a ceremony, like induction into the Army. It doesn't mean a thing."

"I'm that kind of Jew, Dad."

"Sure, honey." He patted my shoulder.

"I like the way the prayers sound."

"Mumbo jumbo. Nobody knows what those crazy words mean. Nobody has, for five hundred years. You want to learn some mumbo jumbo you can put to good use? Learn a few words of Spanish so you can talk to that wetback maid your ma dug up."

"I like Hebrew, Dad."

He looked at me and smiled again. Half a smile is all you get from old Dad. "Tracy Lynn, what will we do with you? You're a stubborn ornery little pigeon."

"You could have put me in the river when you found out I was MBD'd."

"Hush, ya hear?"

"They put Moses in the river in a basket, and a princess found him. You could have put me in the river."

"Don't you let me hear you saying that again." He was mad and pushed me off the chair.

"Julie Olson Banning Anderson Williams gave *her* baby up for adoption. You could have—"

"Shut up, I say."

Talking to old Dad, things turn out that way.

Alan had to miss Bar Mitzvah practice on Monday again, because he had a swimming meet. My mother drove him to Irving, which is sort of close to Fort Worth, so I walked over to the temple to tell the rabbi.

"Hi, Tracy!" The rabbi was so happy to see me. His huge dark eyes light up whenever I come to see him. He's old, about forty-five, and is very nice to me. I think he's always glad to see me because there's never anyone at the temple. That great big praying room that makes me cry because it is so beautiful, you would think there would be lots of people sitting there all the time looking around at the lovely windows, or talking with God. I heard that two thousand families belong to our temple. That's a lot, I guess, even for Dallas. It's too many to fit into the praying room on Rosh Hashanah when they all come. Some of them sit in Sunday School rooms and watch the rabbis on TV. I always go early so I can feel the blue and red sun on me through the window and hear the little whir sound when the Ark is opened.

But when I go with Alan for Bar Mitzvah practice, no one is there. I can't understand it. Don't some of those people in the two thousand families feel the way I do? The room is so large, like the ballroom of a castle, but so much more beautiful that I know for sure that God is there. I've got a spot I like, right in the center, where I can see everything. My spot holds me still while my eyes run all around the room, and I sometimes hear the wind whispering, like my mother, saying, "Tracy, you're in your place."

"Well, well, well, well, *well,* so you've been dispatched to tell me the prince can't make it today, right?" The rabbi always jokes with me.

"He has a swim meet in Irving. He forgot to tell you last week. But he'll be here tomorrow. I promise."

"The question is, will he be here Friday night?"

"Friday night? But that's his Bar Mitzvah night."

"It is! Shall we take bets to see if he shows up?"

"Oh, Rabbi, you're so funny."

"Well, look, if he gets busy and can't make it that night, we'll just make you a Bat Mitzvah in his place."

It wouldn't happen, I know, but I didn't mind pretending it might. "Can you listen to me say the candle blessing?" I asked.

"Certainly, little one. Say it a dozen times—two dozen if you like. Your family has a treasure in you, do they know that?"

Maybe they do, but I don't think so.

We were at the dinner table, just done with the bear claws from Epler's bakery. My mother was smoking her third cigarette. I learned on TV that smoking is very bad for you, that you could die young from it. My mother already coughs. She doesn't watch TV much, because if she did, I'm sure she'd quit smoking.

Alan said, "The presents are pouring in. The mailman practically collapses under the load every day. But Eric is still ahead, and his isn't until the week after mine."

"How many copies of *Roget's Thesaurus* so far?" my mother asked.

"Three, and counting."

"Fountain pens?" she asked.

"Six."

"It's a greedy business," my father said. "I could have bought you a crate of the finest fountain pens in Texas and skipped the whole shindig and still saved about two thousand bucks."

"Then I'd miss out on all the fun. All the guys are doing it, Dad."

"Thank God we didn't have to go through this for Vivian or Tracy," my mother said. "Once is more than enough."

"I talked to Rabbi Feibush today—"

"So what *else* is new," my father said.

"—and he told me to remind you about lighting the Sabbath candles, Mama."

My mother and father looked at each other across the table, until my father started laughing. "My gentile wife is lighting the candles at the Bar Mitzvah?"

"I'm not a gentile," she told him coldly.

"Might as well be." He laughed.

"I'll have to call Feibush tomorrow and get it straightened out." I never like the way she calls the Rabbi "Feibush."

Alan asked my father, "Wanna hear my speech after dinner?"

"Spare me the parts about 'committing myself to the faith of Israel,' and the 'thanks to my beloved mother and father for their undying support.'"

"You really didn't help at all," I said.

"Another country heard from."

44

"Don't you want to hear my speech, Dad?"

"I'll listen to it," I said.

Alan looked at me with one eye squinting. "You? Okay."

"How in the hell am I going to do the blessing?" my mother mumbled.

"Fake it," my father said. They both laughed again.

"I'll do it," I said, so quietly that no one heard.

"Do you suppose Feibush could teach it to me in three days?"

"Doubt it."

"Oh, hell. Who asked for this complication?"

I don't get mad often. I take a lot of medicine that keeps me calm. But I was getting very mad, and when I get mad my head feels like it's going to pop open. I've had seizures before, and that's how I felt just before the seizures, with my head tight and pounding and my eyes blurry. Only this time I wasn't having a seizure. I was just plain angry.

"You don't care, you don't care, you don't care!" I screamed. "Alan doesn't even care." By then my mother had rushed over to me and was trying to calm me, petting me like a kitten. So I yelled in her ear, "I care, I'm the only one, even Rabbi Feibush knows that. I'll do it, I'll do it."

"Do what, Tracy dear?" my mother asked, in her hospital nurse voice.

"I'll light the candles. I'll say the blessing. I don't care if you don't come to the Bar Mitzvah. I don't care if Alan doesn't come. I'll light the candles, and that's what everyone will be there to see."

45

"Call Dr. Akron," my father said quietly. Alan didn't move. "Get up off your ass and get to the phone!" he shouted.

Then I was calm. I showed them. No seizure. I was calm. "I'm okay."

Alan looked at my father, who shouted, "Sit down!" Alan sat down. "Tracy Lynn will light the damn candles."

It was the first time in my life that I won.

Vivian came in from Arizona and brought me a tiny cactus. She told me not to touch it because I'd get prickles in my fingers. But I touched it in my room, and I'm still okay. She went to the sewing lady on the way home from the airport, to see if her dress for the Bar Mitzvah fit okay. My dress was beautiful, golden. I picked that color because that's the color the temple looks with the candles lit. And then I would be behind the candles, and we'd be all one.

Aunts and uncles and cousins came, with a lot of suitcases, and all of them stayed at the Hilton Hotel.

There was a luncheon at Ports O' Call for all the people from out of town. Alan and I got the day off from school so we could go. I ate more for lunch than I usually eat for dinner. We wouldn't have time for dinner anyway. My mother didn't even have time to row that day, and it was her racquet ball day, and she missed that too.

Alan really wanted to shave on the morning of his Bar Mitzvah, but there was nothing to shave.

The flower shop called three times because the yellow roses hadn't come in. Would we take daffodils instead? My mother said no, roses.

United Parcel and Railway Express each stopped at our house two times with presents. Alan didn't even open them. He already had five Kiddush cups and eight boxes of stationery with his name printed on it.

Finally it was time. My mother wore a bright yellow dress that hung from her big shoulders like a tent. My father walked like a king, in a soft gray suit with a vest, and a pale yellow shirt, and his favorite cowboy boots polished so bright that I could see myself in them. The temple was filling up, just like on Rosh Hashanah. People were shaking Alan's hand and straightening his tie and telling Vivian what a young woman she'd turned into since she went away to college.

Rabbi Feibush came to get Alan. "Well, Tracy, how beautiful you are tonight. Are you ready for your co-starring role?"

"Oh, Rabbi, I'm not really a co-star."

"No, my little one, your part is very important. You light the way for the Sabbath Bride."

I guess I just smiled and smiled, because Rabbi Feibush hugged me and sort of crushed the yellow rose pinned in my hair.

And then it was starting, and we could barely see Alan over the top of the speaker's stand. He cleared his throat and nothing came out. Rabbi tested the microphone. Finally Alan found his voice and told all those people watching him that his sister, Tracy Lynn, would bless the Sabbath candles.

School ends next week, and I can find out what's happened to the Horton family since I had pneumonia in March. Dr. Tom

47

Horton has a lot to worry about. One of his daughters died of leukemia. The other one ran away and became a nun. Two of his sons had amnesia, which means they forgot everything that happened to them before they woke up one morning. From now on I will never forget anything that Rabbi Feibush teaches me. There are no rabbis on *Days of Our Lives*. The Hortons aren't Jewish, of course. Dr. Tom Horton's daughter is a nun, don't forget.

No, from now on I will never forget anything.

I don't know how long it will take. Maybe I'll be seventeen or eighteen. But Rabbi Feibush is teaching me, and when we're ready, all the aunts and uncles and cousins will come back, and Vivian will come from Arizona, and they'll be there when I am Bat Mitzvah, and maybe my mother will light the candles that night.

LIGHTER THAN AIR

THEY WERE GATHERED BY BOBBY'S LOCKER, AS THOUGH THEY were furtively planning a heist: whispering, casting glances over their shoulders to make sure no one was in earshot. The Jewish students of Sioux City, Iowa, unconsciously gathered that way, and no more than three at a time. People shouldn't think they were clannish; people shouldn't think they were having secret ethnic meetings. Once Bobby and Charlene and Aaron and Becky and Jeff were all together at a table in the cafeteria. Some tough guy with a nice goyish dimple in his chin came by and said—not unkindly, actually, but said it nevertheless—"Hey, it's the Matzah Ball Brigade!" Things like that gave them a bad name. Bobby imagined a headline in the *Trailblazer*:

ENTIRE JEWISH POPULATION OF TERRANCE HIGH
ASSEMBLES TO DISCUSS CURATIVE EFFECTS OF CHICKEN SOUP
Tomato Rice Doesn't Cut It, Gentiles Told

No, three at a time was the unwritten code. Aaron said, "Did you see Mr. Rhoades today, in the black pin-striped suit? He looks like an undertaker."

"He's too short to be an undertaker," Charlene said. "You have to be long and thin. It's part of their job description. Besides, I think Mr. Rhoades is already dead."

"Right," Bobby agreed. "They stuffed him just so he could teach geometry. At night he hangs on the wall next to a moose."

"Poor Rhoades." Aaron laughed. "Hey, can you pick me up for Confirmation Class tonight? My parents have a vacuum cleaner salesman coming over or something. They can't tear themselves away."

"Oh, Aaron, you can't miss tonight," Charlene teased. "This is the Big Night we've all been waiting for. Rabbi Shuman gets into IT."

Bobby said, "You mean Adolescent Sec-shoo-ality?"

"Quote, unquote," Charlene added.

"Okay, we'll pick you up, Aaron. I've got to go—I'll be late for English."

"English. Ooh, it's too, too divine," Charlene said. "I hear Limey Blimey Blimton's a panic, true?"

"Panic. I've got to go," Bobby said, backing away. He ran his fingers through his hair, or tried to. It was too curly, too tight, like a halo around his face. And his face—too round and angelic for fifteen. When he looked in the mirror, he thought he looked like a monk. Friar Kornfeld, the eunuch. When he looked for signs of thickening hair on his face, there were a few hairs, just in front of his ears, but their encouraging appearance was lost in the smooth, country glow of his cheeks. Healthy, unblemished, like he thought only pure, clean thoughts. How the skin lies!

He stopped short at the door of his English class, as he nearly always did. Someone behind him said, "You finish the paper for Limey Blimey?"

"Sh," the other girl said, "she'll hear you."

"Limey Blimey Blimton," the first girl said, louder.

Mrs. Blimton didn't hear or, rather, didn't look up. Bobby watched her from the doorway. She was writing something on the blackboard, stretching way up to reach the upper left-hand corner—just a trace of the familiar wilted beige lace showed below her skirt. Her hair, a sort of faded red, was pulled back loosely and held with a madras ribbon today. Usually it was a wooden barrette. Bobby guessed maybe her barrette had been lost in the folds of bedsheet, in the tumultuous tumble that surely took place there all the time. It was *Mrs.* Blimton, after all. She wasn't an innocent daffodil. He felt his face flush, and he pulled a handkerchief from his pocket to blow his nose. Too loudly. Everyone looked at him, but not Mrs. Blimton.

"Good afternoon, ladies and gentlemen," she said. "Today

we begin a marvelous adventure, the finest novel in American lit-ra-toor."

"Does she mean *Coma?*" Sandy Chains, next to him, whispered.

"Not *Coma.*" Mrs. Blimton laughed. She heard everything, *everything.* "Not *Rich Man, Poor Man,* or any of the other muck they've adapted for the telly."

He loved when words like "telly" came out. In fact, her English accent fascinated him altogether. It made the language sound so much more authentic, certified. Too bad she was teaching American Lit, not English Lit. Well, nothing was perfect.

"And not *Ragtime,* and not *Grapes of Wrath,* which are both splendid novels, incidentally. No, today we begin *The Scarlet Letter.*" She went to a metal cupboard and grabbed an armload of books. "Help me, won't you, Jason, Rhonda? Pass these out, won't you now?"

Bobby cringed. Why Jason? Why wasn't *he* chosen? The first day, when she was getting used to their names, she'd called him "Baubee," and everyone had laughed. She'd glanced up from the roll sheet, picked him out on the seating chart. Of course, she could have picked him out by the rhubarb color of his face. He blushed all too easily. Country glow run amuck, as Mrs. Blimton would have said had she been asked. Which she wasn't.

"Shall I call you Robert, then?"

Yes, Robert. It was perfect when she said it, so dignified, mature, worldly.

At night, when he was trying to fall asleep, he'd hear, "Oh, Robert, you smell divine."

"A bit of aftershave," he'd reply suavely.

"A spicy scent," her voice would whisper, and he'd feel weird and nervous all over.

"First we've got the hussy, Hester Prynne. She is not a shy, retiring woman, mind. A brazen woman, a determined woman, exceptionally strong, Hester. And tell me, what sort of picture do you get of a man named Roger Chillingworth? Wanda?"

Wanda said, "He sounds sort of cold."

"Precisely. He'd chill you to the bone. Dickens did the same thing with his people, gave them names that told you their most remarkable characteristic. Recall, particularly, Miss Havisham. But back to Hawthorne. What do you think about a chap named Arthur Dimmesdale?"

Maryon Giles, the bookworm, raised her hand. "He doesn't sound too bright."

"You mean dull-witted? Stupid?"

"Well, anyway, dull, dim."

"Yes, you've caught on to Hawthorne's game!" She moved about when she talked. She took short sideways steps, one foot behind the other, and would suddenly be by the blackboard, or in front of her desk, or in the back of the room where someone was sleeping. Bobby never actually noticed her getting there, though he never took his eyes off her. She was just always where she needed to be.

Today she wore a brown pleated skirt and a loose Shetland

tan sweater. To Bobby's frustration, she always wore things that hid her shape well enough so that he could make only the roughest estimates on her dimensions. Adequate, he guessed.

"Robert, what would you guess of the name Pearl?"

He wasn't expecting a question. What did he know about pearls? He stammered,. "Oh, small, round, with a hole on both sides."

Everyone laughed, including Mrs. Blimton. Her laugh sounded like wind chimes, not entirely appropriate to her elegant accent. He was embarrassed to see three hands shoot up around him, as his classmates stumbled over each other to answer the question he'd just made a disaster of.

It was always like that in Mrs. Blimton's. In Rhoades's class, geometry, no one could beat him. American history—boy, the facts entered his head by osmosis. Take the Presidential election of 1888. It was Benjamin Harrison over Grover Cleveland. Harrison lost by 95,000 popular votes, but won by 65 electoral votes. Bobby could do that for just about every election year, and he was very big on the results of battles. But in Mrs. Blimton's class, whatever he read vanished from his memory. Everything he said in her class sounded like wisdom from a bubble gum wrapper, spoken in the most American of twangs, not like her graceful English. Before Mrs. Blimton he had never felt like a Midwesterner, or like a slug. Lower—a flatworm. He was good in biology, too.

Finally the hour was crawling to a close. What a relief when it was over, and he wasn't sitting there with his face flashing red and yellow like a stop sign, and he wasn't going up and down like a yo-yo, and he could go to geometry, where he was sure of the answers. How he welcomed the end of the hour!

How he dreaded the end of the hour, over until one o'clock tomorrow. The twenty-three-hour wait.

"Now, my young friends," Rabbi Shuman began, clearing his throat twice, "tonight we're going to be discussing a subject near and dear to us all, Adolescent Sec-shoo-ality. Of course, I'm not so near to adolescence any more—"

"Not for about fifty years," Charlene whispered to Bobby.

"—but I know whereof I speak."

Bobby suppressed a groan. This was going to be a textbook lecture. Rabbi Shuman, with the long hairs in his nose and about forty years of growing stout around the waist, certainly couldn't remember that far back. He was born a middle-aged rabbi. He came in weighing 190 pounds and wearing a purple velvet skullcap. He couldn't possibly remember what it was like in Mrs. Blimton's class—the unfulfilled expectations, the agony that she or Jeff Rosenberg or, worse, one of the jocks would read the truth on his face and taunt him. Again he saw the *Trailblazer* headlines:

SOPHOMORE GETS HOTS FOR LIMEY TEACHER
The Anguish of Unrequited Love
(*For details, turn to Page 3*)

"—but the fact is, young ladies and young men, your feelings are universal. You can express them freely here.

They'll go no further. Questions?" The rabbi nervously fingered his skullcap, waiting for the first brave soul to reveal his or her innermost longings. There was an underwhelming silence. Finally, out of sympathy for the rabbi's embarrassment, Charlene asked a question.

"Rabbi, what's the traditional Jewish view on birth control?"

It was the perfect question, not too personal, and Rabbi could get off on Biblical injunctions and Responsa literature, ancient and modern, so that everyone could tune out for the duration. It was one of the better Confirmation classes.

"What are you reading, Bobby?" his father asked.

"The Scarlet Letter," Bobby replied.

"Is that the one about the young boy in the war?"

"You're thinking of *Red Badge of Courage,* Dad. We read that in the ninth grade."

"Umm. So what's this one about?"

"Oh, adultery, I guess you'd say."

"Adultery," he tsked. "What you don't find in books today!"

"This one was written about a hundred and thirty years ago."

"Oh, well, a classic, then." He seemed satisfied that adultery was just fine, in the classic sense.

"Mrs. Blimton says this is the greatest American novel of all time."

"Greater than *From Here to Eternity?*"

"I guess so."

"Well, she's English, though. What does she know?"

His father had apparently dismissed Mrs. Blimton. If only Bobby could dismiss her, get her out of his mind, off his face. He absorbed himself in Hester's story, and the nasty little Pearl. He'd know all about Pearl if she ever asked him again.

But the next time she called, "Robert?" it was as if he'd never read the book, never even heard of it. And finally, at the end of the first report period, he flunked English.

"F in English?" his mother roared. "In *English*?"

"It must be a mistake," his father proclaimed. "He's always reading. He can't take out the garbage, he's reading. You think you should go up to school tomorrow, Elaine, and talk to the teacher? Find out what the mistake is."

The way it turned out, Mrs. Blimton refused to see his mother without Bobby's being there. "He's not a child, is he now, Mrs. Kornfeld? We can't discuss him as though he simply wouldn't understand. He has a perfect right to be part of our conference."

This made Mrs. Blimton suspect in his mother's eyes, but full of wonder in his own. Wonder and dread: that she would consider him enough his own master that she would not talk to his mother without him; that she might guess, *know*, and tell his mother why he was a bumbling fool in her class. *Non compos mentis*, incompetent to handle his own affairs. And yet she was saying he *was* competent, that she required his presence for the summit conference even to take place.

"Robert is an exceptionally bright boy, Mrs. Kornfeld."

"Robert? Oh, I know, I know. Straight A's. So why is he failing English?"

"Robert doesn't—Robert, you don't function well in my classroom. You seem—oh, perhaps a bit too meek."

"Bobby meek? Hah!"

"Do I frighten you or intimidate you somehow? I've never meant to, actually."

"N-no, Mrs. Blimton."

"Then I can't guess what the matter is. Is the literature too difficult, Hawthorne too obscure or archaic for your taste?"

"No, it's super, fine. It's all right. It's English, I mean American."

"My Gawd, you're stammering like your cousin Sid."

Mrs. Blimton said, "I think I make him quite nervous. If there is something troubling you, Robert, please tell me or tell your parents. Your parents want to help, I'm certain."

"Certainly we do. You can be sure of that."

"I'm okay, really."

"Not entirely okay, Robert, if I set you off so."

"I'm okay! Why can't you all leave me alone?"

"But you're failing English," his mother said. In her book, failing English didn't mean okay.

"Perhaps we ought to let Robert work this out for himself. I've a good deal of confidence in Robert."

"Yes, yes, we have a lot of confidence in Bobby."

They exchanged smiles. His mother's seemed anxious, he thought, but *hers* settled so naturally into the soft lines of her face that a glimpse of her out of the corner of his eye caused a huge lump in his throat.

"Rabbi? Are you busy?"

"Bobby, Bobby, come in." Rabbi Shuman was surrounded by open books with pencil notes in the margins. He was talking a sermon into the dictaphone. "Come in, Bobby. Always nice to see one of my Confirmation boys. Sit down, sit down."

There were open books on every chair. Bobby moved a stack to the floor, noted the disapproval in the rabbi's eyes, and so moved them back to a corner of the desk.

"I've—uh—sort of got a problem. Not a serious problem. Just a problem."

Rabbi Shuman wore a playful smile. "Maybe I can help."

He's not going to take me seriously, Bobby thought. "It sort of has to do with what we discussed in Confirmation last week."

"Responsa literature?"

"Well, not directly."

"Oh, you mean Adolescent Sec-shoo-ality."

"Well, kind of." Should I or shouldn't I? he wondered. I could go now and leave all the worms still in the can.

"Would you like to tell me about it?"

"Not really, no." He paused. "Well, there's this English teacher. She's crazy about Nathaniel Hawthorne. She's about twenty-four, twenty-five, married. She pulls her hair back, but she's got long bangs that cover her eyebrows, and a feathery smile—"

"You're telling me, Bobby, you're in love with your English teacher?"

61

"No! I never said that."

"No, you didn't." Rabbi Shuman pushed the dictaphone away and lit his pipe, while Bobby sat silently. "Look, Bobby, you're not comfortable talking to me about this. But it doesn't take Solomon the Wise to figure out that you're upset. If we had another rabbi in town, especially a younger man, believe me, I'd send you over. You could use somebody to talk to, somebody you trust. Me, I confirmed your mother and married your parents, and you don't think you can really confide in me, am I right?"

Bobby nodded miserably. Rabbi Shuman was okay. At least he understood that he wouldn't understand.

"But it's eating you up. I was in love once with my Latin teacher, ninth grade. She was the first gentile I ever really noticed. Believe me, I was on fire night and day. I wanted to die. But like the Burning Bush, to my frustration, I was never consumed. Ah, but that was at least a hundred years ago."

"But you haven't forgotten it," Bobby said.

"Forget Miss Katharine Oberon? Can you forget a sunset in the desert? She still pops into my dreams every once in a while." The rabbi checked his tie. "Look, Bobby, I've got a speech to make at Kiwanis. But listen, even with Miss Katharine Oberon burning in my memory, I'm not the one for you to talk to. Call up my friend, Father Martine. Here, this is his number. He's a young—I mean *young*—priest, and it just so happens he's a counselor, college trained, and he owes me a favor, too. He's a fine man. Try him." And the rabbi was slipping out the door as Bobby sat in his office, wondering why he was even considering going to Father Martine, the Catholic priest.

Bobby couldn't see Father Martine, some of him being hidden under the water pipes of the ancient Newman Center at Clark College. What he saw were parts of an open-neck shirt and stiff blue jeans, and quite a lot of hair. Father Martine said, "Can you talk to me while I repair these bloody pipes?"

Bobby's first reaction was anger. He wasn't too thrilled about being here in the first place. And talking to the top of the man's head while he fixed pipes—well, it wasn't exactly the study with the stained-glass windows and the half-burnt votive candles he'd imagined. Then he thought, Maybe it will be easier this way. He didn't have to look at the man, meet his judging eyes.

"The problem is, I'm flunking English."

"Are you a little dumb?"

"No. I get practically all A's."

"It doesn't tally, all A's and flunking English, friend. Something isn't kosher."

"Right. It's my teacher."

"Blame it on the teacher. Well, okay, that's a convenient starting place. Damn! The insulation on this pipe is shot. Hand me that rag over there, will you?"

"It's not exactly the teacher's fault."

"You're starting to make sense now. Male or female?"

Bobby hesitated. "A woman." The word echoed through the white pipes, Bobby thought, *woman, woman, woman.*

But Father Martine didn't hear it.

"Good-looking?"

"What?" Bobby asked. He hadn't expected this sort of question from a priest.

"Is she a looker? A knockout?"

"Aw, not really. But in a way, beautiful. It comes and goes."

"That the problem?"

"You might say."

"She keep you awake nights?"

Bobby stared at the priest's head in disbelief.

"Do you find yourself having imaginary conversations with her—you sophisticated and urbane, she demure, flirtatious?"

"All the time!"

"What does she do to you?"

"She gives me assignments to read. Hawthorne, Mark Twain."

"What does she do to you *inside*?"

"She—she makes me feel like a cocker spaniel, like a stupid, sniveling puppy."

"And?"

"And I can't do anything right around her. My mind goes blank, like I'm a cretin when she's around. I feel like a total mental case."

"It's because you're otherwise engaged, buddy."

"Yeah?"

"Sure. The hormones are raging. What's Nathaniel Hawthorne compared to what you feel pumping through all your blood vessels? Hawthorne doesn't stand a chance!"

"How do *you* know?"

Father Martine slid out from under the pipes. "I'm practically human, Bobby."

"So then, what do you do about it? I mean—"

"Oh, I spend a lot of time fixing pipes, riding bikes. Cold showers help."

Bobby laughed.

"I'm not sending you to the showers, friend. I'm just saying face what's going on in you, don't deny it. Then learn to live with it. You got a girl friend?"

"No." Girl friend—"find a nice girl," his mother said. "A nice Jewish girl," his father added. There were about five remotely eligible Jewish girls in town, and three he'd known all his life, like Charlene. They didn't count. Of the other two, one only liked horses and dogs, an occasional gerbil, but not boys. And the other was nearly six feet tall and built more like a basketball player than the guys on the varsity team.

"So find a girl friend. Or take up crew. Get things under control with the English teacher. Here's an idea. Think of something ridiculous about her, something totally laughable. Then focus on that whenever you think of her. Do you lie around fantasizing a whole lot?"

"Yes," he admitted, reluctantly.

"Well, find a replacement for her. An actress. Olivia Newton-John. A waitress at Sambo's, somebody who's enough out of reach, buddy, that she can't mess up your life. Do what you have to, but get her out of your blood."

"Maybe it will just go away."

"Sure. And maybe God did the Ten Commandments in felt-tip pen." Father Martine stood up, dusting white plaster off himself. Bobby was surprised to see how tall he was. He was maybe six feet four, lean and leggy. He wore high-top Keds. His hair, thin on top, came nearly to his shoulders. It was sweaty from being under the hot water pipes. "Maybe it'll just go away. That's great! Listen, I picked up this little morsel from the Talmud—"

"Talmud? You read the Talmud?"

"You haven't got a monopoly on it, buddy. Anyway, Rabbi Shuman coaches me. He's a real scholar, a cool guy. It's a little line that sticks with me, you know, because it's, as they say today, relevant. It goes, 'Our passions are like travelers: at first they make a brief stay; then they are like guests, who visit often; and then they turn into tyrants who hold us in their power.' What I'm saying is, get it under control, friend."

"Yeah, I'll try. You really—you've been a big help, Father. Can I—well, do you mind if I come back sometime?"

"Sure, come. I might be taking a cold shower when you get here, but hang around." He laughed in a way that made Bobby feel more relaxed than he had in weeks.

He went home to work on it. The most concrete thing Father Martine had given him was the zero-in-on-the-ridiculous idea. He had to find something ridiculous about Mrs. Blimton.

There was nothing ridiculous about her. Her hair? Gentle, squeaky-clean (he imagined), bouncing over her eyes. Her body? Well, nothing definite there, indistinct details, nothing to focus on in those loose, shapeless clothes. Her smile was too soft to be ridiculous, and her accent too lovely, too classical to laugh at. How can you laugh at someone who talks like the Queen? Her name? He'd always hated when the kids called her Limey Blimey Blimton. Blimton. Blimpton. Blimp! That was it. He tried visualizing her as a blimp. Blown up unrecognizably, out of proportion, so full of hot air that when she spoke her words were choked and garbled, like echoes underwater. He pictured her with round, ballooning cheeks, like a Campbell's Soup twin. And if you stuck a pin in her cheek, she'd pop. Only the wilted beige slip—no, not her slip, he'd focus on something more neutral—only the Goodyear blimp gray would be left of her. And blown up, she'd have to be rolled down to the teachers' lounge or out to the parking lot to her VW. They'd have to push her in, stuff her into the front seat. And how would she drive? Bobby smiled to himself at the image of The Blimp trying to reach the gas pedal, or trying to get the pleated skirts and Shetland sweaters around Itself.

Well, it was a start. Not the whole answer, and not even a B in English yet. And then maybe all the ludicrous imagining and focusing would fly to the ceiling like a helium balloon let go, when he actually saw the hair in the barrette and heard her call, "Robert?" But it was a start. And if Hester Prynne could live with it, couldn't he?

Then maybe someday, when he was a senior and growing a Van Dyke beard, and two or three of the Jewish kids gathered at his locker, they'd be able to discuss Mrs. Blimton in the same way they discussed the gnome, Mr. Rhoades, without all his internal organs turning to egg whites. And he'd be able to put three or even ten coherent words together in her presence and think of her without flashing red, even if the beige lace showed a bit.

But for now she was—he needed her to be—The Blimp.

HASTY VOWS

IT WAS THAT TIME OF YEAR WHEN THE LEAVES BURNED GOLD in Missouri. In days past, Jews would go to the river and bathe themselves of their sins to prepare for the Day of Atonement. And old grandfathers would sit on the porch in the last warm afternoons of the year, reminiscing about how they came over on the boat from the Old Country.

"Hurry up, Papa, will you please?" Mona Zebroski bustled by the old man. He never moved quickly enough for her, never talked fast enough. He'd been quick, but that was when Mona and Ben were first married and he, widowed even then, was too quick. Now he spent his days languishing on the

71

porch, wading through the thick, stagnant waters of memories old and untrue. "Come on, Papa, we'll be late for Kol Nidre services."

"Go. Hurry. I'll stay behind if it's so important that I rush myself."

Mona looked at him with impatient affection. "Ben will be home in a minute. He'll expect us to be ready. Lauren!" she yelled.

Papa Zebroski curled up in the porch swing, like a stray kitten. "I'll stay here."

"For God's sake, Papa, it's Yom Kippur."

"How much could I have sinned since last year, an old man like me?"

"Okay, okay, stay. But you explain it to your son. *Lauren!*"

Lauren came out on the porch. "Papa, let me fix your tie."

She fussed over her grandfather, which he allowed for a moment, then muttered, "I can still dress myself."

"Up, Papa." She gently tugged on his arm.

"Up Papa, down Papa, I'm always getting orders. The family mongrel."

A car drove up, not Lauren's father to pick them up, but someone else. It was that boy, Mona observed, that boy Stuart. Mona stared coolly as Stuart walked up the front steps, wearing torn jeans and a yellow Galaxians T-shirt. He was short, with hair nearly the color of his shirt. Mona thought his face was quite empty, his skin and hair and eyebrows all one color. Only now, at the end of summer, there were remnants of sunburn across his nose and cheeks, and a few freckles.

Lauren felt for the wall behind her. Her heart beat so fast with remembered love and anger that she felt weak and needed to brace herself.

"Hi, Lauren," he said easily, as though he came by every day. It had been five weeks and three days.

"Doesn't he know it's Yom Kippur?" Mona whispered.

"I guess not," Lauren responded. Why, after all this time had passed, why had he decided to come now?

"Did you come to sit with me while they go off to repent?" Papa Zebroski asked.

"You going somewhere, Lauren?"

"Well," she replied weakly, "it's a sort of holiday for us."

"Holy day," Mona corrected her. The boy should know what he'd done, sauntering up at such a time.

"Day of Atonement," Papa Zebroski explained. "They swarm to the synagogue and moan and wail about their misdeeds. Then they go out and do it all over again."

"Oh, Papa." Lauren stroked his cheek lightly. "We're going to services, Stuart. What did you want?"

"I sort of thought I'd like to talk to you."

Why, after all these weeks? "I suppose I could call you in the morning."

"You'll be at services in the morning," her mother reminded her.

"I'll call him later then, Mother. You make it sound so impossible to arrange."

"Whatever you think," her mother said.

"I guess I'd better get going." Stuart looked around, seemed uncomfortable for the first time. "I'll talk to you tomorrow, then?"

When he was gone, the old man said, "You've got a cold heart, Mona."

"The boy shows no sensitivity. Coming by on Yom Kippur, my God, no sense. Every calendar tells you when it's Yom Kippur. And after all this time, why does he pick now?"

"Eh," Papa said, shrugging.

Mona was a commanding woman. She wore clothing as though it were leaves on a tree, as though it had grown naturally on her from the inside out. People were intimidated by her grace, her inherent knowledge of what looked smart and elegant. She welcomed this distance between herself and others.

Until the surgery, two years ago, she'd worn her hair pulled into an austere knot—a hairdo designed to keep people away. But after a prominent Kansas City plastic surgeon tucked her face up behind her ears, she'd had to settle for a softer hair style, one that feathered around her face. People thought it was the new hairdo that made her look so much younger, more vibrant. She'd sacrificed a certain elasticity in her uncommon smile, but it was worth losing, so that she'd look ten years younger than her husband instead of three years older, which she was.

"Look, Ben's here. Are you going to services or not, Papa?" Mona knew he would go. He always went to hear Kol Nidre.

"Eh, I guess I'll go. I'll be struck down before my next birthday, otherwise. At my age, that's not such a bad idea."

Lauren took his arm, guiding him down the stairs to the waiting car. Her mother walked alone, her arm on her shoulder bag at just the right angle for *Vogue*.

It was unnerving, Lauren thought, how slowly her father drove. He avoided freeways—death traps, he called them— and took short, choppy city streets nearly all the way across town to the synagogue. Well, at least it gave Lauren a lot of time to think, and what she felt like thinking about was Stuart, at the beginning. June. The Arapaho High auditorium . . .

The curtain came down, thud, bounced up a couple of inches or so, and all the bodies rose from the dead of *Hamlet*, Act V, Scene II. Her best friend, Emmy, pulled Lauren across three people's feet and up the aisle, to be the first to greet the cast. Lauren was about to meet Laertes, or rather Stuart Radburn, the Famous. Famous for Arapaho High.

"You'll just die," Emmy whispered behind her. She was a big girl. She parted crowds in the aisle, and Lauren followed. "He's adorable, beautiful. Since the play he's been around my house night and day practicing with my brother. And really, no kidding, he's dying to meet you."

"What if he hates me?" Lauren whispered.

"Hates you? But I gave you such an enormous buildup. He's probably panting in the dressing room at the thought of your arrival."

But he wasn't panting. He was sweating, and the heavy makeup was drizzling down his face. After eleven years of Senior Plays at Arapaho High, they still hadn't figured out that it would be a hundred degrees in Kansas City in June.

Lauren's first thought was, He isn't adorable or beautiful. He's streaked. And for someone who looked so noble and could duel with a rapier so ably from Ophelia's grave, he was rather short. Still, having been so recently dead, he didn't look too bad.

"Stuart Radburn!" Emmy burst in upon him, then turned to beam at Lauren like a mother who's taken her daughter to audition for a commercial. "Here she is, Lauren Zebroski!"

Well, he was coming down off the high of his vainglorious death. This was probably no time to introduce him to a small girl with plain brown eyes and a nose that looked like it could open a can of tennis balls. Lauren prepared herself for the worst.

"Oh, hi," he said, obviously trying to muster up some enthusiasm.

"You can do better than that," Emmy boomed. "She sat through the whole boring play."

"I thought the play was fine," Lauren said quickly. "You were a really good Laertes."

"I guess I wasn't too bad," he agreed, and Lauren made a mental note: Modesty isn't one of his overwhelming virtues.

Several girls crowded around Stuart and asked him how the makeup felt, did he get nicked at all by the sword, and did he plan to go out for drama in college in the fall. Stuart held court, answering each question with noble patience, while Lauren watched.

Decidedly short, she thought. She couldn't tell much about his hair, since it was so sweaty, and his eyes looked like blue pinheads in all that greasepaint. This sure didn't look like the Incredible Radburn According to Emily.

Suddenly he turned from the admiring throng and shouted, "Hey, Lauren." All the girls turned to stare at her, as if she'd called him. He came over to her and said, "Look, we can't get to know each other in this mob scene. How about I pick you up at eight Saturday night? We'll go to a movie or someplace, okay?"

She nodded, and all the girls glared and probably wondered, Why her?

Mission accomplished, Emmy bustled her away. "You see, he's crazy about you. Did you see the way he was drawn to you in that whole gigantic crowd? You're ideal for each other."

"You think so?" Lauren said doubtfully. Well, not exactly ideal. Aside from his character flaws—five minutes in his royal presence and there were already two big items on the list—but aside from these things, there was one other little item. He wasn't Jewish. For herself, she didn't care. He was a very important person at Arapaho High. He was captain of the debate team, vice president of the Student Council, practically a straight-A student, and he held some sort of track record at Arapaho—fifty-yard dash or something like that. His credentials were absolutely solid. It wasn't at all important that he wasn't Jewish, not to her. But to her parents! She shuddered at the thought of having to tell them.

Lauren's father's voice broke into her thoughts: "You look very dapper, Papa. You too, Mona."

Dapper. Lauren was sure "dapper" wasn't the effect her

mother was aiming toward. Her father did not understand his wife's inherent sense of style. He chuckled when she insisted she wanted to open a fashion consultant business, go into people's closets and advise them on how they could bring a little chic into their lives. Ben owned a dry cleaning business and thought of clothes in terms of seams and nub and stubborn stains. Otherwise, he wasn't interested.

He wasn't a large man. He was about the same size as his wife. And though she scared him just a bit, he thought her the most beautiful woman in the world. Lauren once heard him tell his own father, "I'm a lucky man, a lucky man. A steady income, two healthy sons who married decent girls, a sweet little daughter, a gorgeous wife, good health. What else could a man ask for?"

"Turn left here, Ben," Mona said.

"Next corner, sweetheart."

"You're right," she said. She made concessions now and then, for his pride. He was, for all his unkempt personality, a most gentle, generous man. "You're just like a homing pigeon, Ben."

Lauren listened and recalled the huge amounts of ego-boosting her mother did for her father, as though his ego weren't sturdy enough to support itself. Stuart was different. Ego? He had ego to spare.

And then she thought about that night when she'd told her parents she had a date with him. It was such a typical scene.

"Who is this boy you're going out with?" her mother asked.

Her pencil was poised in the air, and a huge pile of papers stood stacked on her desk. She was Working at Her Desk, which was a ritual she performed every Tuesday night.

"He's very big at school. Debate, Student Council, all that stuff—oh, and a senior."

"What's his name, kitten?" her father asked. He lay on the bed with the TV remote control switch in his hand.

"Stuart Radburn."

"Has he ever been here before, for a party or anything?"

"Mother, you act like I have a party every month. I had one party, last year, and it bombed."

Her mother nodded, remembering. She believed in parties and dancing. It was good exercise. Anything that elevated the blood pressure for a while, brought a blush to the cheek, required planning and coordination, she was in favor of. Lauren was sedentary, more like her father.

"What's the boy's name?" her father asked again.

"I already told you," Lauren yelled.

"I didn't catch it."

"Ben, turn the volume down."

"Stuart Radburn, *Radburn*," Lauren said, struggling to be calm. Nothing to gain from getting them mad. They'd just tell her she couldn't go out with him.

"Do I know his mother?"

"How do I know who you know, Mother!" Calm, stay calm.

"Jewish?" her father asked.

"I knew it. That's what you really wanted to know all along, isn't it? It wouldn't matter in the least if he were an imbecile or had four noses across his face, just so he was Jewish."

"So then he's not," her mother said, in the quiet, grating way she had of summing up the obvious for those members of the listening audience who missed it.

"What difference does it make? I'm not marrying him."

"Good God, I hope not." Her father snickered.

"I'm just going to a movie. One date. He's not going to contaminate me for life," she shouted, and tramped out of the room in a childish way that embarrassed her when she thought about it later.

And later, in her room, she wondered why her parents were so hung up on this religion thing. Weren't all people brothers and sisters? What difference did tiny ideological differences really make? Whether you worshiped on Saturday or on Sunday. Whether you had a Christmas tree or didn't. Whether you went to a church or to a synagogue. Didn't it all end up in the same place, and wasn't He maybe laughing at all His silly children arguing about the one true way to reach Him?

Had her father had these same thoughts when he was a sophomore in college, about to quit to marry Mona Wilkens? And if he did, and if he came to the same conclusion Lauren did, about the religious thing being so unimportant, why then had Mona, her mother, converted to Judaism? Her father wasn't an observant, religious man, and yet her mother had converted to join him and his parents. Why?

And anyway, why was she letting herself get so worked up over a boy who oozed ego and sweated a lot? He probably wouldn't like her anyway. In her sophomore year Gordon Kahn had liked her a lot, but he was building a brilliant future for himself at Safeway, and he'd memorized prices to elevate himself from the puny ranks of bagger to checker. He had a gift of estimating cantaloupe weights. A big night for him was driving by Milgram's Supermarket and comparing advertised prices.

Then there was Dave Rapman. He'd taken her to a disco place and discovered that she had no sense of rhythm, so he lost her in the crowd while miraculously finding Mindy Saperstein. Lauren took the bus home that night. Well, Gordon and Dave were both Jewish. It couldn't be worse with Stuart.

To her great surprise, he showed up on Saturday night holding a bunch of daisies he'd picked from her front yard. He was standing at the door with his hand squeezing daisy juice from the stems, and a huge grin on his face. Somehow his appearance put her at ease.

"Daisies don't smell so good," he said, "but you didn't have any roses out front."

"Oh, thanks." She took the flowers. How come on TV when someone brings flowers, there's always an empty vase nearby, Lauren thought. She put the daisies on a bench in the hall, and they promptly separated and fell in all directions. Stuart gathered them up and handed them to her again, crouched on the floor, and they both laughed.

Her mother materialized in the hall, as she often did when Lauren had company. Lauren handed her the flowers. She knew just what to do; she stuck them in a ceramic mug on the hall table.

"This is Stuart," Lauren said.

Her mother put her hand out. Awkwardly Stuart shook hands with her, and it was almost nice to see Stuart Radburn the Famous not in total control of the situation, for a change. "How nice of you to bring flowers," her mother said.

"I got them—" He stopped, since Lauren had kicked him.

"Be home by midnight, dear. I'll be up writing bills anyway." Her mother took the mug away to the kitchen.

Stuart offered her three choices for movies: an expensive first-run, which he made clear he couldn't afford, something with subtitles, and a pair of *Pink Panther* reruns. She chose the *Pink Panther.*

"You have excellent taste, Lauren Z. I'll just have to keep you around."

"How generous of you," she muttered.

"If you want to stay around," he said.

"Oh. That's different."

The irony, of course, was that she stayed around but he didn't. She should have known the differences were too great. Like that first night when Stuart brought her home. Her mother was waiting by the door and hugged her as though Lauren had just been rescued by helicopter from the frozen tundra. "You're home right on time, dear."

"Of course. I was trained that way."

Her mother smiled her approval. "And what time do you have to be home, Stuart?"

"No special time," he answered, and Lauren watched the irritation cloud her mother's face.

Why couldn't he have said twelve-thirty or one? "No special time" sounds so . . . careless. Mother would see it that way, careless. Anyway, why did Jewish families have to be so protective?

"Well, don't be up too late, Lauren," her mother said, moving up the stairs.

Then later, after Stuart left, her mother came into her room, yawning. "He seems like a nice young man, Lauren. Not too tall, is he? You say he's an actor? Odd. It seems to me he doesn't have much expression to his face. He has sort of a WASPish face."

Lauren knew then that the battle lines were clearly drawn.

Ben pulled up in front of Congregation B'nai Israel. "Help Papa out," Ben said over his shoulder to Lauren.

"I always do, Daddy, don't I, Papa?"

"Eh, with a little help from a crane I could do it myself."

"I'll go park the car," Ben said. There was no place to park in back of the synagogue. It was built in the days when Jews did not drive on the Sabbath or the Holy Days, when everyone lived within a short walk of the synagogue. Life changed. The less observant moved out of the center city, to ranch-style homes in the suburbs. But for the High Holy Days, they returned to the synagogues of their youth. Only now they had to park, lock their cars to protect their tape decks, and walk long hostile city blocks to reach the Eternal Light.

The foyer of the synagogue was bustling with people, some of whom had renewed their annual conversations ten days before, on Rosh Hashanah. There was a tension in the air, foretelling the emotional stirrings of the chanting of Kol Nidre in the strange Aramaic language, and the unaccustomed reflection inward that the poignant melody aroused.

Lauren's friends did not go to this synagogue. The two Jewish friends she had went to the Reform temple close to their neighborhood. As for Lauren's family, when the High Holy Days came, Ben took them back to B'nai Israel and the rabbi who was too old to retire but could only wait to be released from his duties by his Creator.

So Lauren had no one to talk to in the foyer. She leaned against the wall, waiting for her father, and thought about her own confused Jewish education. She'd never gone to Sunday School or to Hebrew School, though her mother had learned Hebrew when she converted. Her mother had flashes of Jewishness—whole months when she'd prepare for Jewish festivals and bake hallah and attend the ritual baths.

Stuart came to dinner one Friday night at the peak of one of Mona's Jewish periods. So there they were around the linen-covered dining room table, in July. Lauren thought Stuart looked very uneasy. He'd told her that at his house they didn't use cloth napkins, and they didn't dine by candlelight. They used paper place mats which his mother rolled into a giant ball at the end of the meal and stuffed into the garbage. Mona would not have approved.

On that Friday night Papa Zebroski pulled out Mona's chair

to help her in. He patted her paternally, for he liked her well enough, but could not bear her excursions into tradition. He himself was disturbed by ritual. It reminded him of the men mumbling words by rote, like so many bumblebees, while people in the Warsaw streets below were gathered and led to the slaughter on their Sabbath.

Lauren knew how Papa felt, and she smiled at him. Stuart, thinking the smile was for him, moved closer. Everyone noticed.

The blessings done, and the soup, Stuart found in front of him a brown thing like an ice cream ball on a bed of lettuce. He pushed it around on his plate, flattened it, found it pasty. He tasted it and nearly gagged, while the others at the table ate theirs with gusto.

Ben smeared his on hallah, so thick that a bite into it left teeth marks. His mouth full, he asked Stuart, "Don't you like chopped liver?"

Chopped liver! Lauren noticed him turn pale.

"It's so nice to have you at our Sabbath table," Mona said.

"It's nice to be here, Mrs. Zebroski," he replied, too politely and wishing he were anywhere else, alone with Lauren.

"Yes, it's an honor to have a young man from *Hamlet* at our Sabbath table," Ben said. "It's the first time, isn't it, Lauren, that we had a boy here for Sabbath?"

"Ben," his wife scolded, while Lauren sank deeper into her chair, blushing.

"What's going to happen to you, now that you've graduated, Stanley?"

"Sir?"

"My grandfather wants to know what your plans are," Lauren said. "And it's Stuart, Papa, not Stanley."

"Stuart, Stanley, so what?" The old man stared at Stuart, still waiting for an answer.

Stuart took a deep breath, already suspecting that the answer would not be acceptable. "Oh, I'll be going to the community college nights and working during the day. I can save up a little and maybe go away to school next year."

Ignoring the "working during the day" part, Mona asked, "What will you be studying in college, Stuart—dramatics?"

Lauren saw the look on Stuart's face and said, "Do you have to interrogate him, Mother?"

"Interrogate? I didn't realize."

"Can't we talk about something else?" Lauren pleaded.

But apparently there was nothing else, because the whole table was silent until Papa filled his wine glass for the third time and said, louder than necessary, "*L'chayim*, to life."

"*L'chayim*," everyone murmured, even Stuart.

In the synagogue they took their seats in the worn red velvet pew. Lauren, next to her mother in the balcony, easily spotted her father in the crowd of men below. Like all the other men, her father wore a small black skullcap, but beside him was Papa Zebroski, who refused to remove his hat.

Mona looked magnificent among the old and shapeless women who sat more as spectators than participants in the Women's Gallery. Since Mona had studied Hebrew, she could follow the service; most of them could not. Lauren read the English translations silently, counting the pages to the end of the service.

A rich tenor voice sliced the air of the synagogue, as the mournful Kol Nidre melody wove itself around the ancient woods and velvets of the sanctuary. For Lauren, the Kol Nidre, more than the triumphant blast of the *shofar*, stirred her to worship. And she tried, but felt ill-equipped to worship well. So she dwelled on the words of the Kol Nidre. They never read the English at B'nai Israel, but she had seen the translation in the mimeographed service from another congregation. The Kol Nidre asked that God release His people from vows too hastily made or made under irresistible pressure. Stuart. They had promised each other so much, and nothing.

An hour passed, and her mind wandered again. Stuart would not have been able to take this if she had gone so far as to bring him here. The words would have made no sense, the rising and sitting at mysterious times even less. If a wedding, a joyful traditional Jewish wedding, caused such a chasm between them, what would this old rabbi lost in the folds of his prayer shawl have unleashed? She thought about the wedding, five weeks before.

Lauren's cousin Estelle is getting married at last. She's thirty-one, and the aunts have feared that her time would never come. But Estelle has found a physics professor, and 246 guests have come to see them joined under the marriage canopy. The professor brings the most expensive shoe he's ever owned down upon a linen-wrapped glass, and all 246 guests know he has shattered the glass as sadness shatters joy, and joy sadness, just as he and his bride will later that night shatter the loneliness each has lived behind.

At least this is what the aunts believe, have always believed, but Stuart thinks the ritual is ridiculous. He comes from that side of life which instinctively knows that breaking glass means bad luck. The splintering glass disquiets him. And nothing in his experience has prepared him for the lavish kissing and embracing that follows.

He falls out of the receiving line and goes outside to the courtyard to breathe. Lauren's aunts have noticed him, with the straight blond hair, the nose that turns up at the tip like an elfin shoe. She hears them talking.

"He's a goy," Aunt Minnie whispers.

"Of course a gentile. What else today?" Aunt Milly replies.

"At least Estelle did okay," Aunt Minnie assures them both.

Papa Zebroski, the family elder, is seated near the door to the courtyard, where he can see Stuart pacing and blowing his hair off his forehead.

Lauren goes to the ladies' room to fume. Stuart has behaved like a child. He could at least be tolerant, even if things are different in his family, his starchy family. In his home a monumental accomplishment, like winning a debate trophy, is rewarded with "That's fine, son." Curiously, that seems to be enough for Stuart.

He's talking to Papa Zebroski when Lauren returns to the

reception. He is squatting at the man's feet, carelessly resting his arm on the old man's knee. He stands up, seeming taller for a moment than she remembered, checks the knot of his tie, and spots her across the room. A waiter offers him more champagne, which he gulps on the way over to her. He beams coarsely and puts his arm around her. "We're here to have a good time, on Cousin Estelle's father, right?"

Lauren raises her eyebrows, still angry.

"Well, then have a sip." He offers the champagne. She turns away. "And introduce me to the famous aunts."

The aunts are twins, but don't look at all alike. Perhaps sixty years ago, when they were young, they did.

"Aunt Milly, Aunt Minnie, this is Stuart."

The aunts eye him and exchange glances, then Aunt Milly says, "So happy to make your acquaintance."

"Likewise, I'm sure," Aunt Minnie says.

Stuart, in a flourish, takes each one's hand and kisses it. "You ladies look ravishing tonight. But then I didn't see you last night. Aren't you proud of Estelle and her Jewish professor?"

The aunts are puzzled, look to Lauren for a clue.

"I think that's enough, Stuart," she whispers in his ear. "We'll see you later, Aunt Milly, Aunt Minnie." She tries to steer Stuart away, but he has grabbed Aunt Minnie and is kissing her on both cheeks, quite noisily.

Mona appears, with a champagne glass poised gracefully in her hand. "Call him off," she whispers. "He's had too much to drink."

Lauren yanks him away and leads him outside.

"Here, wait, let me just break this glass for good luck," he sings, kicking the sliding glass door. And Lauren, in hot tears, leaves Cousin Estelle's wedding to cry in her parents' car.

The next day he doesn't call and she doesn't call, and each feels that to bridge the gap between them means giving up too much.

She misses the nightly phone calls, and the laughing over TV commercials, and the picnics of candy bars and Diet Pepsi by the Missouri River, and his skin, which tastes salty.

He is ashamed, but can't bring himself to call and tell her so. Instead, he dreams, half awake, of her hair falling over his neck and shoulders, nearly as cool as the river wind at night. But the differences between them are unmanageable—the linen napkins, the candles and blessings, the glass that splinters his nerves each time he hears it in his mind.

And then there's that one thing between them that can never be eased away with logic or caresses or Emmy's exuberance. The fact is, he doesn't feel comfortable in her home. It's not that he expects Early American furniture, or a TV set in the living room, as in his house. And it really has nothing to do with the pictures on the wall, except maybe the charcoal rabbi poring over his books. But it's something else—the way her mother surrounds her and questions her and needs to know everything about her. And something smells different in her house: different foods, different soaps. There's no fireplace, no scent of twice-burned wood. But these are such small things, and at the same time so obvious, that he's never brought her home to his house. She's been to his family reunion at a park, though, and met 109 members of the Radburn-Fisher clan. She was overwhelmed, because she said there weren't half that many living members of her own family scattered around the whole world. And the Radburn-Fisher clan couldn't remember her last name.

Lauren feels differences also. He has a grown sister he hasn't seen in three years. Can this be possible? Her own brothers bring their families across the continent to visit twice a year. And then, Stuart's mother doesn't ask where he's going, when he's coming back, where he's been. She trusts his judgment. Or is she just indifferent?

And there is no one like Papa Zebroski in his family, no one with an accent and a different culture and a right he feels he's earned by age to say whatever's on his mind. Stuart's grandparents are from Montana, and they blend into the background like mellow old wallpaper. Their time past, they step back. Papa doesn't and never would.

How can there be so many differences, she wonders, without even touching on the religious one?

The ladies around Lauren began gathering their handbags and hankies while her mother changed from reading glasses to distance glasses. "*Gut yontif, l'shanah tovah,*" the ladies murmured.

Everyone met in the foyer downstairs, where names of the ancestors were remarked in brass on memorial plaques, each with a tiny light beside it.

91

Papa Zebroski had unceremoniously begun his twenty-four-hour Yom Kippur fast, this man who distrusted ritual, because to do otherwise after eighty-two years was unthinkable. He needed a mouthful of water. All about him younger men boasted of their hunger and thirst.

"*Gut yontif*, Papa," Mona said, smiling, for he was her only link to the Jewish past.

He patted her face tenderly. Ben gathered his flock to shepherd them back to the suburbs until morning services. He helped his wife on with her coat, more gently than usual. He kissed his daughter and his father. He was only going to get the car, but he gave them all a long look over his shoulder as if he might never see them again.

Lauren caught a certain expression in his eyes, the protective look of a man not very strong in a family of strength. She felt somehow pulled to him, as daughter or mother, and felt the tug of generations on her conscience. That was what Stuart lacked, despite his 109 relatives—the sense of generations. His people had been Americans for seven generations. He had American Indian ancestors. He was as American as the clay of the earth, and he had no need to look back behind the corpses of World War II, or the destroyed family records, or the Jewish names changed for survival or by an immigration officer who didn't listen well. Stuart knew just who he was. But she and her people were forever unraveling the mystery of their own heritage. She felt suddenly that she rather liked living with the mystery of untold, untolled generations.

And five weeks had passed since she'd last been with Stuart;

the worst of the pain had already passed. Should she allow the chance to be hurt again? Having come so far, after five weeks, shouldn't she just stay with it? Could there ever really be anything for the two of them?

She decided not to call Stuart in the morning. To seal her choice, she silently took her grandfather's hand. They waited together for the car, beneath the lighted names of Papa Zebroski's parents.

STRANGERS IN THE
LAND OF EGYPT

I THOUGHT I'D SEEN EVERYTHING THROUGH THESE LUMINOUS, intensely masculine eyes of mine. I mean, I've been around nearly sixteen years, and not just around here. Everywhere. Wherever there's an Air Base. I've lived in Alaska. Nobody you know lived in Alaska, I'll lay you odds. Or Iceland. Or Austria, either. We only go where it snows. My father can pick the spot, see, because he's a three-star general. There aren't too many Jewish three-star generals, so he names the game whenever he's ready to move on.

Only we don't go where he goes any more; my mom's got custody.

But like I say, I've seen it all. Anyway, I thought I had, until one Friday night when we were waiting for Sabbath services to begin. Once a month we make the scene to keep our hand in. So who walks in but this black family—a mother, a father, and two kids. The guy was about nine, the girl about fifteen, dressed like they're going to hear the symphony do Beethoven. Except for their slightly overbaked shade, you'd have thought they were the Average Middle-Class American Family.

There must have been three hundred people at services. So at least 296 of them shut up immediately after the Grand Entrance. Then everyone started buzzing. The president of the congregation—well, his eyeballs about came unstuck, and the rabbi did a double take and practically knocked over this enormous silver Kiddush cup.

It's not that we never had any blacks in the place before. No, whenever there's a Bar Mitzvah, there's always one or two people of the Black Persuasion. (Black Persuasion: do you like that? It's a catchy little phrase I picked up from someone who told me I was a member of the Jewish Race.) Anyway, the Bar Mitzvah family always has a black friend or employee, or at least a maid, *somebody* to represent the Black Persuasion. Usually the B.P. representatives don't drink the wine for the Kiddush, because they belong to churches where taking a nip is considered immoral. For Jews, it's considered imperative.

But this family I was telling you about, they were different. We could all see that right away. They were nobody's guests. I turned to this guy next to me. He's not a mental dynamo, but he's a member of the Youth Group and therefore better than sitting with my mother and my sisters. I said to him, "Who are *they?*"

He said, "I don't know. The O. J. Simpson family?"

Then the service began, and can't you just picture them getting up and sitting down at all the right places and bowing their heads in holy reverence, etc. Okay, the body language stuff is no big thing. But when all four of them stood up and said, along with the three hundred of us, *"Shema Yisrael,"* well, a hush fell over the whole congregation as though someone had just told a dirty joke in the presence of a nun.

After services all four of them (including the nine-year-old kid) grabbed wine glasses, and the whole congregation chanted the Kiddush. Believe me when I tell you that family knew all the words, as well as everyone in White Sox Stadium knows "The Star Spangled Banner." And then it was clear, all right, even to the lamebrain next to me. These people thought they were Jews!

During the Oneg Shabbat—that's this sort of party we have after services, when everyone stuffs themselves on sweets and punch that tastes like soap—people kept trying to talk to the Average Middle-Class American Family. But it was hard to know what to say. It was socially awkward, even for a guy who's usually very poised, like me. Well, so Roger the M.D. (mental dynamo) and I sauntered over and said something profound, like "Hi."

"Hi," the kid replied. Oh, we were off on a clever conversation.

"Barry Wyman's my name. This guy's Roger Shindler."

Roger M.D. had his mouth packed with cookies, and when he smiled, he sprayed crumbs all over the Average American Girl. She dusted them off delicately, which was when I noticed that her hands were brown outside but actually pink inside.

The father said, "I'm Cedrek Morgen, this is my wife, Mrs. Morgen, our daughter, Esther, our son, Joshua." They all smiled on cue. That trick again: brown lips outside, pink inside. I guess I never noticed that particular phenomenon before in my worldwide travels. Eskimos—I can tell you just about anything you'd want to know about Eskimo anatomy. But these people? So I said to them, "Are you—uh—new to Chicago?"

"Yes, we've just come from New York," Mrs. Morgen answered. She wore her hair in a big sideways sweep that pulled her eye back at the corner. "I was transferred with my company."

"She's an executive," Esther announced.

"Junior exec," her brother corrected her.

"And my husband's work is portable. He's a technical writer, free-lance. So we relocated. Did you grow up here?"

"I'm still growing up here," Roger replied. He's a real wit.

"Not me. I've lived everywhere." I wanted to ask them how did they know the *Shema?* But I couldn't think of a way to ask that wouldn't sound crass. So you can count on Roger M.D. for things like that.

"Hey, are you related to Sammy Davis, Jr.?"

100

I wanted to sink through the floor. But they took it gracefully.

"No," Mrs. Morgen laughed.

"I don't get it. Why Sammy Davis, Jr.?" Joshua asked.

"Because he's black, and he's Jewish," Mr. Morgen replied. He didn't laugh, the way his wife did.

"Oh, I get it!" Joshua said. "Are you guys related to Howard Cosell?"

Roger shook his head no. I just stood there trying to look tall.

Well, so that Sunday our Youth Group met, and in walked Esther Morgan. Roger and I were the only ones who knew her. I figured, like you say on Passover, we were all strangers in the land of Egypt, so I said hello, come in, that sort of thing. But I doubt her people were in Egypt with the rest of us, to tell you the truth.

It so happened no one was sitting next to me (what else is new?), so she plopped down on the sofa beside me. Lucky me.

Sally Farb, the president, said, "Who's this, Barry?"

"Her name's Esther. She was at services Friday night." I did a shrug thing with my eyebrows.

"Hi," a few people murmured, not overly enthusiastically.

Sally called the meeting to order. "Okay, guys, listen up. The first thing we've got to talk about is the Shul-In this weekend."

Esther leaned toward me. "What's a Shul-in?" she whispered.

"It's this thing where everyone brings a sleeping bag to the synagogue, and you stay up half the night talking and playing guitars and stuff—"

"Barry, shut up. I'm trying to conduct a civilized meeting."

"I'm sorry," Esther whispered, and she touched my arm lightly.

We had a black maid once when my sisters and I were small. Her name was Amelia. She used to get us in clinches and hug us until we hurt; a hug from her was a fender bender. I didn't like it. She smelled wet, mostly. Esther's touch was gentle. No bruises. And she smelled like—like applesauce cake, warm and spicy.

Everyone was staring at her when she wasn't looking, then dropping their eyes down when she was. It was starting to make me mad. Okay, I wasn't the most popular kid in the Youth Group. The day I ran for every office but Chaplain and lost, people dropped their eyes when I looked at them, too. They *should* have been embarrassed. They don't know it, but I'm quite an exceptional guy. They could at least let me be treasurer. I can juggle numbers all right.

Then I thought, here we are, the past and future outcasts of the Temple Youth Group, assembled on one sofa. What a target. Okay, she was black, but what did they have against me?

"Barry, stop tossing the tennis ball in the air," Sally commanded.

"Yeah, Barry, you're acting like a nerd again."

"Shut up, all of you," Sally snarled. "We've got a meeting going on."

102

As usual, nothing was accomplished. We had a ten-minute debate over what time the meeting was officially adjourned. I had an Accutron Digital Chronometer on, so you know it was right, but no one paid any attention to me. She leaned over again, Esther, and said, "What difference does it make whether the meeting was adjourned at one-thirty or one-thirty-two?"

Maybe she knew the *Shema*, but she sure was naïve about how the Youth Group functioned.

She was the first to leave. Everyone stayed put until she was gone.

"What's the story on *her*?" Jason asked.

"Who knows? Do you know, Barry?"

"Who me? What do I know?"

Roger, the aforementioned Mental Dynamo, said, "Her whole family was at Shabbat services. Looks like they're Jewish."

"They couldn't be Jewish," Jeannie said. "They're black."

"There aren't any black Jews?" Eric asked.

"Of course not. Look at the facts, stupid," Sally Farb said.

"They could have converted," Jason suggested.

"No," I said. It sounded sort of loud, even to my own ears. Well, you have to be loud to get attention in this unruly mob. "This is no quickie conversion case. They look like they've been doing all this stuff for a long time."

"It just doesn't make sense. Who ever heard of a black Jewish family? It's bizarre."

Then Esther did a really underhanded thing. She threw the

door open and burst in on our private conversation. I noticed that her brown cheeks were sort of reddish. You could almost see the flames shooting from her mouth, too.

"All you smart-assed kids, you don't know a thing, do you?"

We all just sat there, stunned.

"All you super-Jews, listen to this. My parents and grandparents and great-grandparents were Hebrews, descendants of the Falashas of Ethiopia. You've never even heard of the Falashas, have you? I'll bet you don't even know that Abraham, Isaac, and Jacob were all black." She stood in the center of the room, spinning one way and the other to pierce each person's face with her eyes. She was small but powerful. "You can all be Jews, converts; we are Hebrews." She was breathing fast. Her shirt was sort of palpitating. She wore a short Afro, almost heart-shaped around her face. Funny, as mad as she looked, I still wanted to go up there and pat her hair. I couldn't decide whether it would be coarse and woolly or soft as duck down. Would it flatten when I touched it or pop back up? Of course, I controlled the impulse, because the next thing, she was saying, "I was Bat Mitzvah two years ago. Can all of you say that about yourselves?"

"Only the girls," I quipped.

She spun around and glared at me. "Then the rest of you ought to have an instant replay on your *brisses*, because I don't think they *took*." Then she stamped out of the room, nearly breaking the window on the door as she slammed it.

Then everyone was glaring at me, as if it were all my fault

that she'd been sneaking around eavesdropping outside the door and having a whole public fit.

Finally Eddie Fieldman said, "Any of you guys got a lawyer in your family? This chick's probably going to file a discrimination suit against the Congregation Beth Am Youth Group."

"Jeeze, Barry, look what you've done *now*," Sally said.

People like me, we're the scapegoats of the universe. One of my sisters is eighteen. If a guy takes her out once and doesn't call back, it's my fault. "You grossed him out, Barry, just by being yourself."

My other sister is thirteen, a budding adolescent, and she blames me for her straight hair. "You got all the wave, Barry. There was nothing left over for me." I'm accused unjustly. First of all, what she knows about genetics would fill a nostril. Second, having wavy hair like Liberace is no real asset. It hasn't done me much good. But I'm blamed.

So it wasn't a big surprise to hear that the Youth Group blamed me for Esther's tantrum. I could have predicted that, if I'd had time.

At lunch hour the next day I faced her. Not faced her—she wouldn't look at me—but I talked to her. "It sure seems like you got out of joint at the meeting yesterday," I began. Maybe it wasn't the most diplomatic way to proceed.

"Oh?" she said icily. She was with a girl friend, black, who wore tiny crosses for pierced earrings. I noticed then that Esther didn't have holes in her ears. Again I wanted to pat her hair, but her friend, a head taller and six shades darker, stood guard over Esther.

105

I motioned to the Bodyguard. "Is it okay?"

"Mantha knows the whole story," Esther said. Her eyes were small, dark dots, not sympathetic eyes. I know sympathetic eyes when I see them. Not forgiving eyes, either, I suspected. Boy, if she'd been in the Warsaw ghetto, she'd have been organizing the Resistance. But the Germans would have quickly picked up that she wasn't of pure Aryan stock.

I said, "Those guys in the Youth Group, they don't know any better."

"What's your excuse?"

That's what my mother always used to say. "You were supposed to have dinner cooked when I got home. What's your excuse?" It's a trap, you know. If you come up with an excuse, it's never good enough, and then, by definition, it's only an excuse.

Once I said to my mother, "The reason Dad left is because you couldn't ever get anything done around this house, and you weren't even working then. What's your excuse?" She hit me, the first and last time. Then followed a lecture on the complications of male/female relationships, which I wasn't old enough to understand yet (being a very worldly fourteen), and besides, I had as much to do with his walking out as she had. She was blaming me! I wanted to remind her that I wasn't the one who was married to the guy, but it still stung, where she'd slapped me. Later, much later, she apologized and told me she'd said all that stuff because she was sad. That cleared the air, and we've gotten along pretty well since.

"What's your excuse?" Esther repeated.

I shrugged my shoulders. "I don't know. I like to make jokes?"

"Very funny."

Mantha smirked and turned away, so I moved in a little closer to Esther. "I was sort of hoping we could be friends." Mantha and Esther looked at each other. Mantha nodded no.

"No way," Esther decided, on cue.

Big Mantha was making me good and nervous. "Can I talk to you alone?"

"What'chu need to talk to her alone for?" Mantha demanded.

I tried to ignore the daggers she was shooting my way and whispered to Esther, "Could I come by your house after school, iron it all out?"

Esther glanced at Mantha. She was obviously at a crossroads. It was something like: Do I stick with my girl friend against this guy? Or: Do I stick with my black sister against this honkie? Or: Do I stick with my black Christian sister against my white Jewish brother?

"Come by after five," she said simply. Mantha gave her a disgusted look and walked away.

Her house was a lot nicer than ours. We live okay, on a general's alimony, in a high-rise apartment. But we're only on the fourth floor, and she lives on the eighteenth floor of her building. She can see clear to Indiana from her window. There were boxes stacked all over the white fluffy carpet of her living room, because, as she explained, her mother works about twelve hours a day.

She took me in to see her father, who was sitting at a large wooden desk. His den seemed to be the only room in the apartment that was settled. It was a cavern of book-filled walls. On one bookshelf I saw a turquoise seder tray, the kind that's made in Israel. The one wall with no books was nearly covered with framed line drawings—Picasso, Miró, Ben Shahn. The guy had taste.

"Dad, this is the boy you met at Temple Friday night. The one I told you about."

"Um-hm. I remember."

"He says he wants to make amends."

Her father pushed his typewriter table aside and stood up. "Perhaps we're an anomaly to you."

"Sir?"

"Anomaly. Something unusual. An enigma."

I barely caught what he was getting at.

"Are you assimilated Jews, your family?" The man talked like an encyclopedia!

"Oh, well . . " My voice trailed off.

"By that I mean does your family blend right into the lives of your neighbors?"

About ninety percent of the people in our building were Jews. The doorman was Jewish. I didn't understand what he was trying to say.

"Do you play ball on Saturday, eat at McDonald's, sing Christmas carols in school? I can see at a glance you don't wear the traditional fringed garment. I'm willing to bet money, young man, that given a choice between going to the synagogue or going to a football game, you'd be in the bleachers."

"Yeah, well, I'd have to agree there."

"That's what I mean by assimilation. You're not recognizably different from the larger population around you."

I nodded, tried to look intelligent, but that sharp-eyed girl saw through me.

"My father means we're assimilated too, into the white community. We live in a mostly white building. My mother has a high position with a white corporation. My brother and I don't go to ghetto schools, or speak the cool dialect, or eat fried pork rinds." She grimaced at the thought.

"Okay, I see that."

"Barry, is it?"

I nodded. "Yes, sir."

"Barry, the intriguing situation here is that we've come to be wholly accepted into the white community. But in the synagogue it's a horse of a different color."

"Oh, Dad, that's a good one." Esther smiled, but it was a thin smile with not much joy to it.

"I guess I see what you mean, sir."

"What I *mean*, Barry, is that Jews, who've always been the object of derision and injustice, just can't accept blacks in their flock yet."

"But we're not used to it."

Mr. Morgen said, "There are more than forty thousand

black Jews in this country. Get used to it, Charlie."

"We will, but give us time."

"He does have a point, Dad."

I couldn't believe she was actually making a concession. So I jumped right in to take advantage of it. "You see, we've never met Jews—like you before. It's hard for us to believe, at least at first, that you're Jewish. You don't look Jewish." Maybe I'd get a smile from him.

"We are Jewish," Mr. Morgen said quietly. "My father and his father before him—all Jews, from generation to generation."

"My father gets very dramatic," Esther apologized.

"I've got work to do," he said gruffly.

Esther and I went into the kitchen. I was hoping she wouldn't do something like pull gefilte fish out of the refrigerator. Even blacks don't have to be that Jewish. Anyway, she gave me an apple, and we crunched at the kitchen table.

"I didn't understand before," I said, my mouth full.

"Sure, I know."

"You want to come back to the next Youth Group meeting?"

"Um, I don't think so, no."

"Yeah, come on."

"No." She shook her head. "I made a total fool of myself. Not that I'm sorry. You all deserved everything I said." Her eyes softened, and I saw for the first time that I'd been wrong; they were forgiving eyes, after all.

I don't know what came over me. She looked so wispy, so vulnerable, with her reddened cheeks and the piece of apple stuck to her face. I leaned across the table and—well, I kissed her. She didn't even have time to close her eyes. I know, because mine were open. I'm not going to tell you it was a big passionate moment and that violins suddenly burst into a sonata. It was more like—friendship.

I don't make friends easily.

"Thank you, Barry," she said softly.

All I could do was smile and flick the apple off her cheek.

"Barry has a date, Barry has a date," my sister Polly sang in her obnoxious nasal twang.

"It's not a date."

"Barry has a *date*?" My older sister couldn't believe it. She tells me I'm cut out to be a recluse, like a poor Howard Hughes. The truth is, I'm a very social being; I just don't get along with people very well. Take ants. Ants intrigue me. They're so social, so cooperative. They've got it all worked out so well—who does what, who tends the home fires, carries the food, builds the ant hills, warns of the coming of the aardvark.

That's the trouble. There are too many aardvarks in my life. Like Sally Farb.

The Youth Group had a baseball game with the Temple Board, as a fund raiser. I said I could play second base. Well, I screwed up. I missed the catch, a fifty-eight-year-old member of the Board of Trustees got by me. I finally recovered the ball, and while he was ten minutes away from total cardiac arrest, he limped past third base as I tossed a wild ball to Richard

Berger on third. Sally Farb, our duly elected leader, swallowed me alive.

"You incompetent lummox. We've got thirty dollars a run riding on this game." She blew her whistle in my face. She figured it was the president's privilege to wear a whistle around her squatty neck. "Hey, get somebody alive in here on second base. Send Wyman to the showers." You can see why she got elected. Such charm, such pizzazz. Also, she was the only one crazy enough to run for the office.

So I trotted off, grinning, doing the champ routine with my arms over my head. Nobody's going to know what it feels like inside me. A few adults clapped weakly to support me, and my mother was standing there with a pained expression on her face, because mothers are too sensitive about their kids' getting hurt. I slapped her on the back like a pal, to show her I was okay. She'd probably have felt a lot better if I'd put my head on her shoulder and cried my eyes out. But, of course, that couldn't have happened. Then I saw Esther, standing off to the side of the crowd eating a Popsicle. (The Youth Group made four cents on each one we sold.)

"You all right, Barry?"

"Yeah, sure."

"That bitch really let you have it."

I shrugged.

"Want the other half of my Popsicle?"

Boy, was she ever Jewish—consoling me with food! Her tongue was orange from the Popsicle. It always made my mother feel faint when one of us had a wild tongue. A white tongue was the worst. It meant we'd get prunes for dessert until the magic worked. My mother was very attuned to tongue shades.

"Why do you hang around people like that?" Esther asked.

"Like Farb? Eh, they're my friends."

"With friends like that, who needs enemies?"

"I think I've heard that line before." I'd just about finished my half of the Popsicle and was wishing she'd offer me the rest of hers, which was now melting into rivulets and streaking her dark skin with sticky orange. We sat down on the grass, away from everybody, and talked. She listened to me! After a while I found out I didn't have to be such a wit. She'd listen to regular stuff too, like about my father sending me a leather coat for my birthday, and it being two sizes too small because he probably couldn't remember how tall I was any more. I'd never told anyone about that; not even my mother knew how I felt about it. Then I asked her, "You want to go out sometime?"

"Sure," she said gaily.

"Saturday night?"

She hesitated. "Okay. But—"

"What?"

"It's not a date. We'll go dutch treat."

I've always been tight with my money; what luck! But the truth is, her saying that made me sort of sad. She was putting all these disclaimers on the product before it was even sold.

"I mean, it's not like we're *dating* dating," she said. "Just going out somewhere together."

"Oh, yeah." Once before I'd asked a girl for a date. She said *no* in record time. I was getting the same thing from Esther, wasn't I? Just with the speed slowed down. A 78 RPM *no* at 16 RPMs.

So my sisters were entertaining themselves with the great news that I, Barry Wyman, was stepping out. My mother knocked, came into the bathroom where I was experimenting with various hair tonics and sprays. I could achieve a certain suave plastered-down effect with Alberto VO 5, but did I really want to look like an undertaker? That's the trouble with wavy hair.

"Who are you going out with, honey?" my mother asked.

"Oh, a girl."

"Thank the good Lord. I thought it was a boy. So who is it?"

"A girl from school."

"A nice girl?"

"No, Mother, a barracuda."

She smiled in the mirror. We were the same height, but I was darker, like my father.

"I'm not trying to pry, honey, but it's a big moment in a mother's life when her son has his first date."

"It's not officially a date."

She nodded. My mother is always seething with questions she tries not to ask.

"She's a girl from Temple."

"Oh, really? Have I met her?"

I took a deep breath. If I told her, she'd burst a blood vessel. If I didn't tell her, I'd feel rotten all evening. "Esther Morgen," I said, almost in a whisper. Maybe she'd hear it wrong, and that would be the end of that. But not my mother.

She picks up sonar and ultra-high frequency only a dog would hear.

"Esther Morgen. Sounds familiar. Esther Morgen. Esther—" Her eyes grew huge. She grasped my shoulders. "The black girl?"

"Yeah."

She swallowed. I watched about twenty expressions cross her face, until she said, "I hope you have a nice time, honey. Don't be too late."

"At least she's Jewish," I said, and my mother and I had a good laugh.

The scene was not so cozy at Esther's apartment.

First, a Puerto Rican maid answered the door and asked me something in Spanish that I couldn't understand. Esther's mother and father were seated in the all-white living room at the end of the hall. They seemed remote, like decorations in their own home.

"Have a seat," Mr. Morgen said formally.

I perched on the end of a footstool.

"Barry? Esther's mother and I are a trifle confused."

His wife studied me, puffed on a cigarette in an ebony holder.

"Sir?"

"What exactly is your interest in our daughter?"

"We're friends, sir. We talk to each other."

"My husband's not making himself too clear, Barry." She seemed so much softer than he. I relaxed a bit, until the Drill Sergeant spoke again.

"We don't approve of your dating Esther."

"We're not actually dating."

"Call it what you will."

"Oh." I nodded. They thought *they* were confused? I was the one who was confused. "Why not, sir?"

"You and Esther are from two different worlds."

"Excuse me, sir—"

"Please stop calling me sir."

"Yes, Mr. Morgen. But look, we go to the same school, Esther and I, we know the same people. We both like orange Popsicles." That was supposed to make them laugh; I could always make people laugh. But it didn't save me this time. It failed like a parachute that doesn't open after you've jumped. I'd already jumped. "We understand each other, sir. She listens to me, I listen to her." I paused. He glared at me, too polite to interrupt, I guess. "How can you say we're from two different worlds, Mr. Morgen? We both live in high-rise apartments, have parents who are professionals. We're both Jewish, aren't we?"

"You are white, and Esther is black."

So, with all their assimilation talk and the Puerto Rican slave and the cushy executive position, they were still prejudiced!

"What he means is—" Mrs. Morgen began.

"What I mean is, you are white and Esther is black." The veins stood out in his head, and suddenly I felt dizzy from all the white carpeting and white drapes eighteen floors above Chicago.

I began tentatively, "Then all that stuff you told me, the

things you said about being assimilated, accepted into this community, that community, it was all—a crock?"

"Not a crock, Barry," Mrs. Morgen said gently. "But there are still barriers we're not yet ready to tear down."

"Esther's not going out with you tonight, you know."

"I see." I felt nauseous, afraid I'd throw up my dinner on their white carpeting. Out the window there were countless windows of other apartment buildings projecting too high into the sky. I had to get out, felt trapped like a hamster in a glass cage, with the walls too smooth to scale. I ran for the door, and they stayed seated on the white mohair sofa as I slammed the door behind me.

I couldn't go home. Polly and Susan would be full of the questions my mother would have the good sense not to ask. Like why had I bombed out on my first date?

So I walked a long time. I saw what I'm sure was a dope exchange, and two thin strays scrounging for garbage behind a restaurant. I turned down Michigan Avenue, passed the Art Institute, the Chicago Public Library, several travel agencies that promised worldwide adventure and international brotherhood. It was so much simpler when we lived among the Eskimo.

Finally I caught a bus home. My mother was out in front of the building waiting for me, with Polly. Polly didn't say a word; she'd never been so quiet. We were silent all the way up in the elevator. Then, with the door to our apartment closed behind us, my mother threw her arms around me. "Barry honey."

"What's with the big receiving line downstairs?" I asked. I probably sounded hoarse, from hours of speaking to no one.

"Esther called here. She told us what happened."

"I'm sorry, Barry," my sister said.

"I'll survive."

"Esther's calling back about eleven. She sounds like a nice girl, honey."

"Easy come, easy go," I said. I paced the living room waiting for the phone to ring, hoping it wouldn't, wanting it to. Easy come, easy go, says the guy who feels like mud and slime inside.

Finally she called. "I'm sorry, Barry."

"It's okay. Not your fault."

"I was afraid this would happen."

"Your father's a tough old bird."

"My father. He's so full of liberal talk. Until it comes down to the real thing. He's just talk. He's afraid—I don't know—afraid I'll be polluted or something."

"Your mother seems okay."

"Yes, it's easier for her."

We were both silent.

"Barry?"

"Yes?"

"Can't we still be friends? See each other at school and Temple?"

"Oh, sure," I said heartily, but I wasn't sure. I was like her father. Just talk.

"I'm going to try the Temple Youth Group again," she said.

118

"By the oddest coincidence, I'm dropping out."

"Oh, Barry, no."

"Maybe next year, when Farb gets out of office. I don't need her."

"There's so much bitterness in your voice, Barry. I haven't heard that in you before."

"I haven't had my face stepped on before, like I did tonight."

"Sally Farb does it all the time."

"The hell with Sally Farb."

"Barry, about the leather coat from your father—"

I was sorry I'd told her. I should never have let my guard down that way, to get socked in the gut. Sorry I'd told her, sorry I'd kissed her in her kitchen, sorry I'd asked her to go out with me.

"—how you feel about the coat and your father and all. I'm glad you told me. It gives me some perspective on my own father, you know? That's what friends are for, helping each other out. That kind of thing."

"Yeah, I guess."

"I need a friend."

"Oh, you've got one. You've got Big Mantha."

"I need a real friend, a friend who's a boy, a friend who's Jewish. I need you, Barry."

"Do you?"

"Without you, who would eat the other half of my Popsicle?"

"Or the other Hostess cupcake?"

"Or the other half of the Almond Joy?"

"Who would lick the second beater full of frosting?" I caught myself. It would have to be at my house; I'd never go to hers again.

"And if Noah built an Ark tomorrow, in downtown Chicago, who would I walk in two by twosy-twosy with?"

"Oh, great. There's your father standing at the door of the Ark waiting to hog-tie me for the trip!" We both laughed. The knot in my stomach was beginning to dissolve. So I said, "One thing I've been wondering about. Is your hair stiff, or fluffy?"

"I can't believe this, Barry. I've wondered the same thing about yours. It's so wavy and thick on your head. I've never seen that kind of hair close up before."

"Okay, here's the moment of truth, members of the listening audience. My hair is—stubby and coarse."

"Mine's soft and fluffy," she said.

"Oh, well, we can't all be perfect, like me."

"Friends?"

"Friends."

"Good night, Barry." My mother and both my sisters were hovering outside the open door and saw, I guess, the large smile spread across my face.

FRAIL BRIDGE

T HE TRUTH IS, WHEN BUBBIE YETTA DIED, I WAS RELIEVED.
Everyone was relieved, I know, but no one else would admit
it. Maybe it was easier for me because I was a young girl,
sixteen, healthy. I had forever to live, while my parents saw
that they were next in line.

Bubbie Yetta was my father's grandmother—not his mother, his *grandmother*. She was very old, eighty-six, I think.
She'd outlived all her children. When the last one died, my
great Uncle Hersh, she more or less crawled into herself for
good.

On the day Bubbie died, Mama came home, brushed past

123

me as though I were a floor lamp, and headed straight for Papa. She took his hand, which she hardly ever did, and said, "Honey, Bubbie's gone. She went in her sleep this afternoon. I was there."

Papa closed his eyes and nodded.

"Bubbie's gone?" I asked. At last! Nearly six years she'd vegetated in the Hebrew Home for the Aged, and all those years Papa had struggled to pay. I hadn't been able to go to camp since fifth grade because of it. And then, nearly every Sunday afternoon, when I wanted to be with my friends, we were there at the nursing home, visiting. What for? Bubbie didn't recognize us when we were there. It was depressing. All those old, old people sitting around dressed for a party they'd been to twenty years ago, or strapped into their wheelchairs, waiting for their two o'clock pills. I hated going there, and she never even knew I was there when I *did* go. Mama went nearly every day to feed Bubbie her lunch and hold her cold, twiglike hand. I couldn't touch her. My father would say, "Kiss Bubbie, Rachel," but I couldn't bring myself to do it. To me she was already dead, and no young person should be asked to kiss death.

"One thing you can say for Bubbie, honey, she was always a lady, even toward the end. She was always modest." Tiny Mama, who could wear a blouse open to the third button with flair, could appreciate modesty.

Papa was silent.

"You want me to call Bess and Art? They'll need time to get here from Toronto. Also Eva and Fred. I'll call them, honey."

Papa nodded. They were acting so strange. My mother was *never* so gentle. She usually said, "You want something done well, do it yourself, Smarty Pants." Now she was offering to call Papa's brother and cousin to tell them about Bubbie?

And Papa, the shouter, so silent! Finally he said, "I'll start at once to make the arrangements. Get me Sinai Mortuary, Muriel, on the phone."

Mama didn't say, "The phone's right by your elbow, Henry. Is your arm in a sling?" Instead she looked up the number and dialed, while I stood there wondering what was expected of the great-granddaughter of the Deceased.

Aunt Eva and Uncle Fred arrived within hours, and later my second cousin Bess and her husband—all Bubbie's grandchildren. Bess had the right clothes for the occasion. She brought properly subdued colors, not too revealing, but soft and feminine. I thought she must keep a special funeral wardrobe. Aunt Eva sat in our living room, hemming a navy blue dress she'd bought on sale in anticipation of Bubbie's funeral.

The doorbell kept ringing, with people remembering to hush their voices when they gave instructions for reheating the casseroles they'd brought. Apparently the great-granddaughter of the Deceased was expected to handle kitchen duty. Mama came into the kitchen as I was rewrapping a sponge cake Mrs. Shon had sent over.

"Rachel, you have something to wear to the funeral tomorrow, something that comes an inch or two below your knees?"

"I'm not going to the funeral, Mama."

Mama decided to ignore my remark. "Rabbi Orbach from Denver is due in at nine o'clock. I'll have to go and pick him up at the airport. You'll stay here and take care of things?"

"Why can't Rabbi Kravitz do the funeral? He's our rabbi, isn't he?"

"He is. Together they're doing it. You see, Rabbi Kravitz didn't know Bubbie when she was alert, lively. He only knew her when she moved here to San Francisco as a feeble, sick, forgetting old woman. That's the way you knew her also, I'm afraid."

"I'm not going to the funeral, Mama."

She sighed. "Henry," she called, in a weak voice. "Henry, come in the kitchen a minute."

My father, a small wiry man who usually walked in small leaps, seemed to drag his feet into the room. He wore a skullcap, which I never remembered seeing him wear except in the synagogue. "What is it, Muriel?"

"She says she's not going to the funeral."

"You're going."

"I don't see why I have to go." I pouted.

"Lower your voice," Papa said. "This isn't for Aunt Eva and Uncle Fred."

"I hardly knew her," I whispered. "She didn't even move here until she was senile and barely recognized any of us."

"So because she was my grandmother, that's reason enough. Your own flesh, your ancestor back four generations."

"I'm not going, Papa, because I don't believe in death."

"She doesn't believe in death, Henry." Mama was smiling, for the first time since she'd told Papa that Bubbie was gone.

"Enough of that existential crap, or the voodoo, or whatever you call it." Papa was warming to the subject. "You don't have to believe in death, Rochela, because it finds you even if you've got your head buried in the sand. You think you're immune? Believe me, it runs in the family, death. Look, both Bubbie's sons died before they saw sixty. And Uncle Hersh lost the twins, Leona and Lillian, at birth. And my Aunt Sarah, too, she was no more than seventeen when she passed away. You think if you don't believe in it, the Angel of Death will pass you by, like from Passover? Forget it, Rochela." To Mama he said, "She'll come."

And I did.

Then after the funeral Mama and Papa and I, and Aunt Eva and Uncle Fred, and Bess and Arthur (Uncle Hersh's daughter and son-in-law) all came back to our dreary house. Usually the sun streams in through the living room, and light bursts into color as it hits the mirror over the couch. But all the mirrors in the house were covered.

Since Bubbie's children and brothers and sisters and her husband were all gone, we were her closest mourners. So we were the ones who sat on cushions and low stools on the floor, our shoes off. No one knew what to say. Finally I couldn't stand the silence any longer. "Uncle Fred, why didn't Larry and Louis come?"

Aunt Eva, so much larger than her husband, answered for

him as always. "Larry is in his first year at Yale. He couldn't take off. Louis is just too young for this—this tragedy."

Bess said, "Art and I discussed it and felt the same. Marian's only eleven, and Billy's only nine. Just too young for this."

I'm too young too, I thought, but I am here.

"Larry should have been here," Papa said. "He's the first great-grandchild. He should have taken off."

"What do you know, Henry—you never went to college," Aunt Eva said.

"Larry should have been here," Papa repeated. "Bubbie used to be crazy about him."

Aunt Eva said, "Remember when he was born? Bubbie came on the plane from Denver."

"Do I remember!" Bess said. "I must have been a girl of nineteen, twenty. Bubbie'd never been on a plane before. Only for Larry she flew. She thought she was going steerage from the Old Country. Fred and I—remember, Fred?—we met the plane. Off she waddles with a bandana over her head, and the orthopedic shoes, and the thick silk stockings, and the dress to her ankles, nearly."

"And the shopping bags, remember, Eva?" Uncle Fred stood up to imitate Bubbie staggering under the load of the shopping bags.

"What did she have in the bags, Uncle Fred?"

Aunt Eva answered, "Cookies. Mondel brot, kichel, honey cake, cherry knishes, all for the *bris*."

"She thought we didn't have a bakery where we lived."

Bess said, "Oh, and I loved when she saw Larry for the first time. She spit three times over her shoulder and said, 'Is this a little *mamzer!*' "

"Naturally, I didn't take offense. I knew my son had a father." Uncle Fred beamed.

"It's just an expression, Fred, just an expression," Papa told him. Papa always seemed to brush his brother-in-law off. Everyone did. It was hard to take Uncle Fred seriously.

"Then," Aunt Eva said, "little Larry still in diapers, there's Muriel ready to produce Bubbie's second great-grandchild, Rachel."

"Did Bubbie come out from Denver on the plane again when I was born?"

"No." Mama said it with such finality that it hurt.

"Why not?"

"Well, there was no *bris*. It wasn't necessary for her to make the trip."

"I see."

"Besides," Arthur said, "Bubbie was always a little tight with the pennies."

"You think so?" Papa asked. "Did you know, Arthur, what she did for my father, your Uncle Morris? When my father went to work, Bubbie was already a widow. She made Morris pay hefty room and board, just as if he lived in a regular boardinghouse. Then, when my father and mother got married, Bubbie took out from under the mattress two thousand dollars that she had saved from the room and board. That was their wedding present, which wasn't bad money in those days."

This was hard for me to believe. Years ago, on my birthdays, I used to get a card from Bubbie (unsigned, for she never learned to write) with a dollar bill in it. My other grandparents always sent a check for twenty-five dollars *and* a gift a girl would love. Bubbie never gave me gifts.

Papa got up off the stool and took some papers out of the bottom drawer of the credenza. "Listen, I don't know if this is the right time, but—uh—"

"Not now, Henry."

"Sure, why not now, Muriel? Years ago, when Bubbie went into the nursing home, she asked me to write something down for her. She didn't take anything with her to the home, a few changes of clothes, that's all." He read over the paper silently. "So she told me to Rachel, her first great-granddaughter, was to go her wedding ring and her pearls. What else did she have, really?"

Bubbie wanted *me* to have those things? Not either of her two living granddaughters, or Mama, who'd been so good to her? Why me? She hardly knew I existed.

"She said from the earliest, her Rachel had *rachmones*."

"Do you know what *rachmones* is?" Mama asked.

"Not really."

"Compassion. A soft heart. Bubbie saw that, even when you were a little one."

Where had that *rachmones* gone? Why was I feeling no grief, no sorrow, at the passing of my great-grandmother? No compassion, even for my father, who must have loved her very much. Or for my mother. My mother had sat with her while Bubbie died a little more each day.

"Ah, I wish my Billy had a little *rachmones*," Bess said.

Had Bubbie noticed me through all those long, boring visits when her vacant eyes reflected nothing? Did she see deeper than I thought? Did she know me, even though I didn't know her at all?

"Billy runs here and there, never tells me where he's going. A mother could die of worry from such a kid."

Did she *know* all those times when I couldn't kiss her, when the thought of putting my lips to that sallow flesh made my stomach churn? All those times that I assumed, because she didn't speak, she couldn't hear, wouldn't understand?

"You know," Arthur was saying, "those beady eyes never missed a thing. I remember right after the war—"

I remembered when she'd come for Sabbath dinner a year or so after she'd gone to live at the home. She sat in a straight-backed rocker and barely moved before dinner, until someone—me, I think—took her to her chair in the dining room. I could touch her arms; that's all I could bring myself to touch. Mama tucked a big linen napkin into the collar of Bubbie's old-fashioned jersey dress.

Papa said, "Let us welcome the Sabbath Queen in joy and peace." Bubbie's eyes looked empty, as usual. Mama put a delicate handkerchief over her hair, then, as an afterthought, went to find one for Bubbie. Mama began the blessing over the candles, and Bubbie started mumbling something.

How rude, I thought. She doesn't make a sound for six weeks, and all of a sudden when everyone's supposed to be quiet and respectful, that's when she picks to mumble. And I remember thinking, I hope I die before I'm fifty. I don't *ever* want to get old. Then I noticed that Mama had stopped the blessing and was listening to Bubbie. The old woman mumbled by rote, "*Asher kidshonu b'mitzvosov, v'tzivonu l'hadlik ner shel Shabbos.*"

"Ah, Shabbos around Bubbie's table. It was really a groaning board." Uncle Fred smiled.

"At least three starches, and the delicious high-cholesterol fat floating at the top of the chicken soup, and the roast chicken falling from the bones. Um!" Bess was wallowing in memories of Bubbie's dinners.

"And she'd come around the table," Arthur said, "with the gigantic ladle from Rumania, and she'd plop a not-so-delicate portion on your plate and say, '*Eat!*' At Bubbie's table you *ate.*"

"Were you at our house, Muriel, the night Louis choked on a piece of bread?" Aunt Eva asked.

I remembered that night, only because I thought my baby cousin Louis was dying. I was four years old. Aunt Eva went chalk-white, and Uncle Fred said, "Oh, my God," and seemed frozen in place. Isn't somebody going to do something? thought little Rachel. Baby Louis will die. Maybe he's already dead. And he'll shrivel up and get eaten by worms in the Hebrew cemetery.

"So Bubbie got up and socked him in the gut," Uncle Fred remembered. "She didn't know from this fancy new Heimlich Technique for choking. She knew only if she knocked the

132

wind out of him the food would come out, too."

So *that* was why she socked him. To little Rachel it seemed like a cruel thing to do—hit a baby because he was choking. That's when I started being afraid to kiss Bubbie, I think. To me, the child me, she was as close to death as Baby Louis had been. Maybe she'd died and come back, too.

Arthur said, "How lucky Rachel is. Bubbie's been here since Rachel was a small girl. Our Marian and Billy, way in Toronto, hardly knew her."

I hardly knew her myself—didn't they see that? And the more I listened to my relatives, the more I realized that what I knew of her, had always known, was wrong.

Everyone was silent for a moment as we listened to a guest at the front door. The women of the congregation were handling visitors and phone calls. We heard a man with a deep, craggy voice say, "Tell Henry a *minyan* will be here first thing tomorrow morning to say *Kaddish*." He lowered his voice, and we had to strain to hear. "When the time seems right, give Henry this note, will you? Mort Goodman found this, from some guy in the eleventh century."

A woman stepped tentatively into the room to give Papa the note, which he pocketed for later. No one questioned his judgment, for he was now the oldest member of the family.

Then Bess seemed to be thinking out loud. "I was so embarrassed when she showed up at our wedding looking like a refugee. Art's grandmother, you know, is a native American. Oh, not an Indian, of course. She wore a regular three-piece chiffon, matronly, like a grandmother is supposed to look. But

Bubbie came in like a field marshal, organizing the wedding pictures and the buffet table, in a black print with more cleavage showing than Raquel Welch, more than anybody wanted to see, believe me."

Mama nodded. "As Bubbie always said, 'From me you get only Yetta Fein. You want a fashion plate, you go to Sexe Fit Evenue.' "

Everyone laughed, until Uncle Fred said, "Hey, this is a funeral, right? Not an Irish wake. We should be a little more respectful and not talking about cleavages."

Papa got very angry. "If it makes us smile and laugh to remember, so it's okay. Even in the Talmud it says not to overdo the mourning. Remember the life of the woman, which God knows she lived each day, as long as she could. Don't just remember the dying." He pulled from his pocket the crumpled note Mr. Goodman had sent. "Bachya ibn Pakuda, from the eleventh century, said this:

> " 'Life and death are brothers. They live in the same house. They are joined to each other and cling together so that they cannot be severed. They are united by the two ends of a frail bridge over which all created things must travel. Life is the entrance; death is the exit.' "

"So she went out the exit," Arthur said. "Well, everybody goes out that way, sooner or later."

"Art is such a philosopher," Bess said. Everyone was quiet for a while, until she said, "Remember young Aunt Sarah?

134

She was always such a mystery to me, dying so early that way before any of us knew her."

I'd always heard about young Aunt Sarah and Bubbie, and how they were more like sisters than mother and daughter.

Bess was saying quietly, "They looked a lot alike, those two. They used to jump rope, can you picture it?"

How sad Bubbie must have been when her Sarah died.

"Get us a Bible, Muriel. Maybe we should read from Lamentations," Arthur suggested. "Bubbie always loved a good lament. It was in her soul."

"Yet she wasn't one for talking about love," Mama said. "I can't remember once her ever telling me, or even Henry, she loved us. Do you, Eva?"

"No, not really. She didn't say much about love."

"Words, only words," Uncle Fred said. "What she knew about love wouldn't fit into a sentence, not in English *or* Yiddish."

"Where did she learn about it, I wonder," Mama mused.

"Zaida never talked love either," Aunt Eva said. "But the two of them together, like cement. Nothing could crack through; they were a solid wall, the two of them."

"Where did they learn it, though?" Mama asked again.

"Maybe they were madly in love when they got married," I suggested.

"Hah!" Papa said. "They met for the first time under the wedding canopy, she a girl of thirteen, and him already twenty-six. They didn't look at each other the whole ceremony. The first two years they barely spoke to each other."

135

"But when we were growing up, they were in love, don't forget. Like I've never seen before or since," Aunt Eva said, staring at her husband.

"If only Marian and Billy could have known her like you did, Rachel. She slept here in your home even sometimes, didn't she?" Bess asked.

In my *room*. And when she spent the night, an icy chill fell over my room. After she was gone two days, I'd still pick up the perfumed scent of the dime-store powder she covered her face with in splotches. And when I looked in the mirror, the one she used to powder her face, I saw my own—pinched and drawn and old—in seventy years.

And now the mirrors were covered.

Then I knew I had to see once more. I startled everyone by running out of the room. I had to see what I'd find in my mirror. I pulled the sheet off the mirror and at first couldn't force myself to look at the cold glass, cold as Bubbie's cheek.

Finally I lifted my eyes and saw myself: brown hair around a small chipmunk face. And I saw her too, gaunt, frail, grayish, in infinite reflections going back, back. Then her face and mine folded into one another, like a paper fan, locking with a tiny metal clasp that shimmered in the mirror.

Mama came in as the face in the mirror began to cloud with tears.

"I knew you'd find your tears for Bubbie sooner or later," she said. "Mine I spilled last night in bed, with your father."

"I don't know why I'm crying."

"What does it matter why? It's enough you're crying."
Mama put her arms around me.

And I knew I wasn't crying because I'd lost Bubbie, but
because I'd never had her, not as the others had. I'd never seen
her healthy and loving, moving briskly, ruling the family. I'd
never seen her with her hair down around her face, never seen
her sit on the floor, or stretch from a step stool to reach
something on the closet shelf. I'd never seen her young.

Except then, in the mirror, when she'd looked like me.

ABOUT THE AUTHOR

Lois Ruby, a librarian and Temple youth group leader, grew up in San Francisco. She wrote *Two Truths in My Pocket* using observations she made while working as an advocate of teenagers in various parts of the country. Ms. Ruby now lives in Wichita, Kansas, with her husband, who is a clinical psychologist, and their three sons.

Lois Ruby's first collection of short stories, *Arriving at a Place You've Never Left*, was an ALA Best Book for Young Adults. *Publishers Weekly* praised her novel, *What Do You Do In Quicksand?* (Viking), as "an amazing feat. . . . With all its serious aspects, the story boasts the leavening of unforced comedy and involves readers wholly with recognizable humans."